THE NEXT ROOM

THE NEXT ROOM

Sarah Harrison

Severn House Large Print
London & New York

This first large print edition published in Great Britain 2006 by
SEVERN HOUSE LARGE PRINT BOOKS LTD of
9-15 High Street, Sutton, Surrey, SM1 1DF.
First world regular print edition published 2005 by
Severn House Publishers, London and New York.
This first large print edition published in the USA 2006 by
SEVERN HOUSE PUBLISHERS INC., of
595 Madison Avenue, New York, NY 10022.

British Library Cataloguing in Publication Data

Harrison, Sarah, 1946-
    The next room. - Large print ed.
    1. Single mothers - Fiction
    2. Ghost stories
    3. Large type books
    I. Title
    823.9'14[F]

ISBN-13: 9780727875464
ISBN-10: 0727875469

Printed and bound in Great Britain by
MPG Books Ltd, Bodmin, Cornwall.

One

It was early spring when we moved to Arbury Road, but you wouldn't have known it. There was nothing green there. Except us.

As we walked from the van to our new front door I held Hannah's hand, pretending that it was to reassure her, although in fact it was me that needed reassurance. Jesus, she was nine years old – she still thought that whatever I did was okay, that she'd be safe with me. When I was at school some wretched visiting vicar told us that the word 'faith' had two meanings: belief, and trust. As a child this had been a big 'so what?', but it must have had some resonance because I'd remembered it; and since becoming a parent I'd come to appreciate the terrifying implications of someone having faith in you. With my record, I was the last person anyone should have believed or trusted, but Hannah did. At least till something better came along. From time to time over the years the sheer terror almost drove me to God, so I could pass the buck. Almost, but not quite. It took something a lot bigger and scarier than maternal responsibility to do that.

I had the key ready in my pocket as we approached the door, but the lock was awkward, and I had to let go of her hand so I could jiggle both lock and handle till everything synchronized. Inside, the floor of the narrow communal hallway was littered with junk mail – minicab firms, pizzerias, double-glazers, Indian takeaways, pashmina outlets – plus a few brown window-envelopes. Everything had the air of having been there for some time. The hall was dingy and airless – it didn't matter, it wasn't ours, but I knew this first impression would lower Hannah's spirits.

'You and I better get out here and smarten things up when we're settled,' I said.

She nodded, polite rather than enthusiastic. She looked peaky and anxious, but I wasn't sufficiently confident myself to go into an it's-going-to-be-great routine.

Instead, I said: 'Come on, what are we waiting for, this is ours,' and opened the door to our left.

To my relief, the flat still looked okay – no

better than I remembered, but certainly no worse. And, at last, space! Here, we had a couple of good-sized rooms, linked by a long passage, with a small kitchen and bathroom located halfway between the two. Hannah wandered into the living room, which overlooked the street, and I followed her. The décor was old-fashioned furnished-let neutral, and there was a grey tideline round the edge of the beige cord carpet, testament to years of imperfect hoovering. Sunlight filtered through glass smeary from hasty, last-minute cleaning. We had a gate-legged table with two slatted chairs (company not encouraged, then) a tweedy two-seater sofa-bed with wooden legs, one matching chair and a squat armchair covered in brown Dralon. In one corner stood a bony standard lamp with an old-fashioned parchment shade, and a hundred-watt bulb with a similar shade hung from the centre of the ceiling. The seat of the brown armchair had no give – when Hannah sat on it she perched like a garden gnome on a toadstool. She grimaced and gave a tentative bounce – nothing.

'Feel free,' I said. 'In fact, you have my permission to stand on it and jump up and down.'

She got up. 'It's okay thanks.'

I knew I mustn't let her mood infect me. This might not be homely, but it was an improvement. I went round to the other side of the table and looked out of the window, which was framed by unlined cream linen curtains, hanging like two bedspreads from their wooden pole, the only concession (and that a utilitarian one) to modern style.

Arbury Road was almost indistinguishable from a hundred other residential roads in north London. Like them, it took its tone from its wider surroundings – the vast council estates that loomed before and behind, each block fancifully named after a famous British lake: Coniston, Derwent, Lomond – the railway line a hundred yards to the north and the touchy, unstable poverty of the bustling High Road to the south. No trees – that was a test. In another part of town there would have been some token trees stuck at regular intervals along the pavement, a bit of foliage to assuage the English middle-class yearning for greenness.

As I watched, a couple of youths in beanies and parkas, trainers like spaceships, came along the pavement with that gait peculiar to their kind, part slouch, part strut. I kept my eye on them: the hired van with our entire life in it was parked in a pay-and-display bay a few yards away. They looked at one or two other cars, but passed the van as if it wasn't there. I felt a perverse disappointment – everything I owned, and not worth a second glance.

Hannah was standing in the middle of the room with her hands linked behind her head, as if she didn't know what else to do with them.

'What happens the other end?'

'Come and see.'

She followed me down the passage which, in this early Victorian house, was like a canyon, dark and high-sided. The bedroom at the back had one window overlooking the central area, in which domestic detritus, smells, altercations and disparate musical tastes converged and were trapped in a whirlpool effect. The room was an extension, and its redeeming feature was a skylight in the flat roof. The glass was grimy, and spattered with bird-droppings and leaves, but it still afforded a view of the sky. I pictured myself lying here when, as was often the case these days, I was unable to sleep, gazing at the stars.

Hannah sat on the edge of the double bed. 'Are we both sleeping in here?'

'Yes.'

'What,' she asked doubtfully, spreading her hand out over the mattress. 'In here?'

'No, no – you'll be in the little bed. The one we brought with us.'

'Oo-oh!' Her voice took on an upward, whiney inflection, which I wasn't in the mood for.

'Speaking of which,' I said. 'We should start unloading our stuff.'

There wasn't much 'we' about it – and I had vastly underestimated the difficulty involved in moving in. Getting out of our old place that morning had been a doddle – we'd been fresh, Anita and her partner Janine had helped, the mood had been quite festive. But now it was late afternoon, we were both tired and hungry and I felt the encroaching shadow of depression, like a thumbprint on my mood. Anita, bless her, had said she would come over after work, not with Janine this time but with Kenny from the office, but that wouldn't be for at least an hour. We couldn't just sit about and wait for them. A better parent would have involved her child in the exercise no matter what the inconvenience to herself, but the time, effort, and psychological wear and tear involved in selecting items of the right size and shape which my daughter was then prepared to carry, and keeping pace with her while she alternately dawdled and dashed, was, I decided, too great. Easier by far to dispense with her 'help'. I told her to stay where she was, staggered in with the TV, stuck it on the table and parked Hannah in front of it. The picture was lousy, but after some token griping she settled down on the sofa, soothed by the familiarity of the programmes, the same here as she would have been watching at home. Ah—! I caught myself out with that 'home'. Home was here now.

Doggedly I trudged back and forth. It was mostly boxes – kitchen stuff, ornaments, CDs and videos – and cases with our clothes and personal possessions. The folding camp bed had little casters at the side so you could roll it along next to you, but it was still one hell of a job getting it up the step, and the mattress seemed possessed by the spirit of a homicidal anaconda. The whole exercise was further complicated by the need to lock and unlock the van each trip. My back hurt, I was getting sorry for myself. I decided to find the box containing tea, coffee and biscuits, and get the kettle on, but remembered just in time that the van would need moving.

I had it till the next day, but the maximum parking in one place before six thirty was two hours, and I'd run out of time.

'Hannah – come on, I've got to move the van.'

Her eyes never left the screen. 'Okay.'

'No – I mean come on, you have to come with me.'

'Why? Can't I stay here?'

'Of course not.'

'Why?'

'Because I don't know how far I'll have to go, and I'm not leaving you alone.'

'But I only want to—'

'Hannah!'

'Grrr!' She got up.

'And turn it off, please.'

'Grrr!'

'That's now, if you don't mind.'

I checked that I'd got the house and flat keys before opening each door and then again before closing it. Hannah gave a display of exaggerated patience. I prayed that there would be another space within hauling distance of the house.

There was – in fact one had miraculously opened up in the next bay, so all I had to do was roll forward. Hannah's relief that there wasn't to be a major expedition did not prevent her from making her point.

'I could have stayed there.'

'But I wasn't to know that.'

Back in the flat I located the 'Basic Supplies' box and got the kettle on, in what the agency had described as a 'galley kitchen'. In other words, it could accommodate one undernourished person at a time, provided he or she remained sideways on. It was still more than I was used to. There was one narrow sash window, overlooking the area, and facing the back bedroom. It was odd, looking across into a window that was also one's own – like stepping outside one's self. I could picture Hannah and me in there, me making the bed, Hannah's face gazing out...

After we'd had our cuppa I set Hannah to putting books on to shelves, and prepared to complete the van-emptying. It was a pleasant surprise, when I opened the outer front door, to find Anita and Kenny were on the pavement, debating whether this was the right house.

'Look no further,' I said. 'This is it.'

'Did *you* ever fall on your feet!' exclaimed Anita, gazing around as if at some vista of Capability Brown's. 'It's so great round here!' She'd left Woolloomooloo as a teenager, but a decade among fellow expats in

Earl's Court had ensured that she became resident professional Aussie at Small World, the student travel agency in Handley Street where she oversaw us unadventurous Poms.

Kenny, a cautious fellow, ventured no opinion. 'Hallo, Fee.'

'Hold it right there,' I said. 'No-one comes over the threshold without carrying something.'

'Fucking right!' said Anita. 'Bring it on.'

I led them to the van and opened the back. It was fantastic the difference the extra pairs of hands made. In one fell swoop, the remaining job was more than halved, and my morale rose. Quite apart from their usefulness, having my friends there had the effect on me that watching her programmes had had on Hannah – it restored a sense of normality. We might be in a new, strange place, but there was plenty that would stay the same.

'Where's that daughter of yours?' asked Anita as we staggered across the hall.

'Don't worry, she's here.'

'Nita! Yay!'

Kenny and I exchanged an empathetic look as Anita received the hero's welcome due to a visitor who was not related, swore freely, and wore Ugg boots in all weathers: it was a look that agreed there was no justice. Now of course there was no question of Hannah's remaining in the flat, she was all eager co-operation, so the four of us trooped back out and scooped up the last load.

When it was in, and the two doors locked behind us for what I hoped would be the last time that evening, Hannah dragged Anita and Kenny on a guided tour while I disinterred the Jacob's Creek. They spent a good five minutes in the bedroom – let's face it, that was the only other place to go – and when they came back, Anita said:

'Cool bedroom, Fee. It's fucking enormous and that skylight's the dog's bollocks.'

I ignored Hannah's expression of pure delight. 'Good, isn't it? It's pretty much what sold me the place.'

'But you don't own it, right?' asked Kenny, who was of a literal turn of mind.

'She meant metaphorically, dumbo.'

'I wish it *was* mine,' I said, smiling at Kenny. I handed out the wine, and diet coke – a special dispensation – for Hannah. 'Anyway – cheers, guys. And thanks for your help.'

We clinked glasses. Anita's glance strafed the living room, then narrowed as she spotted something. 'You've got a bit of damp there, you know that?'

'No.'

She went to the party wall, the one adjoining the next house, and drew an outline with her finger. 'See?'

'Oh dear.' I hadn't noticed it before, but she was right; there was a small patch, not much bigger than her hand.

'Nothing to get worked up about, could be a leak in next door's plumbing but you better tell them. And the landlord.'

'I will.'

'It's nice though, Fee, really. Once you've got all your bits and pieces sorted.'

I agreed, uncertainly. I could feel tiredness creeping back. It had been a long, long day and it wasn't over yet.

'We're not going till you're unpacked, you know that?'

'Yay!' said Hannah. 'Can they spend the night?'

'No,' I said rather too emphatically, and then realizing that might have sounded inhospitable, added: 'Where would they sleep?'

I had mixed feelings about the two of them being there all evening, but they were great. By nine o'clock the beds were made, the empty boxes were stacked by the door, the kitchen was functional and Kenny had got in a takeaway from the British Raj. Better yet, the water was hot, and after marmite toast Hannah had had a bath and joined us in her nightie.

'So where's the school around here?' asked Anita.

'The one Hannah's going to is about a mile away – between here and work. It's nice – you liked the look of it when we went there, didn't you Hannah?'

Bad move. She wasn't going to oblige. 'No I didn't.'

'That's the style,' said Anita, 'you've got to hate school, it's in the job description for any girl with half a brain.'

Hannah was mollified, though she wasn't sure why.

'Anything lined up for the weekend?' asked Anita. 'Hot date?'

I gave her a 'fat chance' look. 'We'll be settling in.'

'Fancy lunch on Sunday?'

'Yay!'

'That's really kind, but I don't know—'

'You have to eat. And if you settle too much you'll turn into sludge. See you both any time after one.' She turned to Kenny. 'What about you, fella?'

'Love to but I'm digging.' Kenny was a keen amateur archaeologist.

'There you go, he's off making mud pies all day, you have to come.'

Anita had the vices of her virtues. With the energy, the commitment, the loyal and robust friendship came an invincible bossiness. I had been railroaded, but that was fine.

After they'd gone Hannah proclaimed that she would *never* be able to fall asleep, and did so within five minutes of her head hitting the pillow. I would like to have done the same but I needed an interlude, however brief, to myself, to recalibrate and make room in my head for all the changes we'd wake up to.

I switched on my radio, already tuned to Classic FM, and put it on the table. I turned the overhead light off, so there was only the pale pyramid of light from the standard lamp, not enough to do anything by, but there was nothing more I wanted, or felt able to do. I sat on the tweedy sofa with a spare pillow behind my back and my feet up on the arm. The music, the mournful slow movement of a clarinet concerto, trickled through the room, round and over me ... For the first time since arriving here, almost seven hours ago, I was aware of the actual presence of the place. We had stood around and made our comments and spoken arrogantly of making it habitable with the paltry accessories of our short lives, but beneath the utilitarian blandness this was an old house; a house that had seen people come and go. For well over a hundred years it had given shelter, seen celebration and sadness, endured neglect, indignity and war.

Now, it was oddly quiet. There seemed to be no traffic in the street and, for that moment at least, no-one passing by. No sound from the houses on either side, nor the flats above and below. I entertained a sudden, unsettling picture that we were quite alone – not just in this house, but in the whole street. Could such a thing happen? Was it statistically possible for all the inhabitants of a street to be out at the same time?

I lay very still, straining my ears for a sound beyond the music. I could have switched it off, but the sensation of the very walls, the fabric of the place watching me kept me very still. It was only when the music ended, and was replaced by the comforting rustle of the audience, that I swung my feet down and went, as I was so often compelled to do, to check on Hannah.

She was spark out, with that dogged, almost fierce abandonment of hers. In sleep she positively exuded confidence. In the same way I'd taken her hand earlier, I sat on the edge of the bed to take comfort from her. Now I could hear the distant yelp of a police car and, closer at hand, the chatter of Bangla-rap from another flat.

I lifted my head and – yes. There beyond the skylight were the quiet stars, looking back at me. Just as I'd imagined they would.

Two

We'd lived near here before, long ago. 'We' were my parents and myself; I was an only child. The thinking nowadays is that only children do better – they're more mature, and even better mixers, because of all that individual attention – but I wished, *longed*, for a sibling, or more specifically a sister, to share my secrets with. Because oh! I had secrets, and they were a dreadful burden to me.

I called my mother by her Christian name, Julia, because I'd been brought up to do so. It must have sounded odd and radical to others, but to me, who knew no different, it was the same as calling her 'Mum'. Looking back, I can see that it was an affectation on her part, and also a mechanism by which she distanced herself from her maternal role. She had no aptitude for what's known as 'parenting', and said herself on several occasions that she was glad our father hadn't wanted a son, because I was 'all she wanted'. She wasn't alone in this. Before choice became a right, there must have been thousands, millions, of reluctant parents, mothers especially, and they all muddled through. Now that I had Hannah I could see that muddling through was the name of the game. You gave it your best shot and hoped that with time and maturity your children would understand and forgive.

That said, Julia hadn't muddled through – anything but. She was what's known now as a control freak who managed her job (part-time receptionist, but still), her house, her family and her time with forensic efficiency. My friends' mothers thought her *wonderful* because she did so much and still had time to ferry us to after-school activities, cook like a pro, look *soignée* and keep a difficult husband happy. They didn't know she had no option – she was a woman in flight.

My father was certainly difficult, but not in the way people thought. His name, ironically, was Fairweather, Miles Fairweather. On good days Julia called him Milo. I called him Dad. He was a journalist on a London listings magazine, doing reviews, celebrity interviews, that sort of thing. Sometimes he and Julia would attend premieres, and parties where the guests were stars. Dad was handsome in a louche, baggy sort of way. Someone once told him he looked like David Essex and he never forgot it; he wore his dark hair long and curly with that not-recently-washed look, affected a five o'clock shadow and collarless shirts. His public persona was one of affability on legs; not a mean bone in his body; to the point of spinelessness some people said. His habitual expression was a rueful smile, his posture a hands-in-pockets slouch, his favourite gesture an aw-shucks running of the hand through his wavy locks.

On the face of it, he was the opposite of Julia. She controlled, managed, ran things, was the very model of a modern working mother. His style was laissez-faire. His manner proclaimed that there was nothing left for him to do, so he might as well lie back and enjoy it. It was a chicken and egg situation. No-one could tell whether Miles's indolence was the cause or the effect of Julia's hectic busyness. Only I knew the truth about them, and I couldn't tell anyone because it was too awful. Small wonder I've been a lifelong loner.

Dad was a fair-weather man in more ways than one. I'd say he was a split personality except that that would take responsibility out of the equation and to this day I hold him responsible for his actions. No-one could inflict that much pain, so carefully and consistently, without meaning to – without having fantasized about it and worked out how to do it.

Of course, the first time I heard something I didn't know what it was. It was the middle of the night, the small hours when I awoke; my eyes flicked open automatically; I was instantly alert. The landing light was on and the door was open a chink, just enough for me to see the cabbage-patch dolls on my duvet cover. Their chubby, beady-eyed faces, smiling blankly, looked slightly sinister.

For a moment there was silence, and then from downstairs I heard the scrape of a chair, and a bang. My father's voice, quite low, but insistent. No answer from my mother. Another bang, which I recognized as the sound of the kitchen door crashing back against the wall – it had a tendency to do that, as the scar on the paintwork testified. I could make out a rustling and scrabbling, as though my parents were picking things up off the floor. My father's voice again, this time I caught the word 'perfect' and then, more than once, 'nothing'. But most of what he said was indistinguishable, a drone, as if he were talking to himself.

For a moment I was confused rather than alarmed. Then there was another bang, and a rattling sound as though someone had bumped into the fridge.

I thought: *He's hitting her.*

And then: *No!*

The phrase 'in denial' was not then yet in common currency, but it exactly described my state of mind. Nothing in my small universe had prepared me to accept what I had just thought.

That was the first time in my life that I experienced real dread, like rank, black water seeping through me, filling me up, oozing into my throat as bile and out of my eyes as tears.

I sat there staring at the chink of light in the door. I listened, furiously, all the tendons in my neck stiff with the effort. At last, after a long, long silence, there was the sound of a tap running, water splashing, the familiar clunk of the chairs being pushed in around the kitchen table, the key turned in the back door. My father said, quite distinctly this time: 'You go on, I'll finish up down here.'

I didn't hear Julia's reply, but in a moment there were her footsteps on the stairs, steady and measured.

Shivering with shock, I slipped down under the bedclothes. I held my breath and my heart beat in my ears fiercely. The chink of light was extinguished as Julia paused by the door, and then it broadened and softened as she opened the door and stepped over the threshold.

For a child, there is no awfulness like the shattering of the accepted order. All manner of things are tolerable if they are the norm. I didn't want my mother to come any closer, I didn't want to see anything that would justify my new and terrible fears. I lay deathly still.

But Julia didn't come closer. The only

sound my straining ears detected was a minute, wet, intake of breath, like the inhalation of someone with a cold. Then she stepped back, the door was once more pulled to, and a minute later I heard the bath taps running. From downstairs came the swish and rattle of the sitting-room curtains – Sanderson's Country House, my mother's pride and joy – being drawn back. As my father came up the stairs, I heard the latch on the bathroom door, on the other side of the landing, slide home with a click.

He popped his head round the door as he sometimes did. Often, if I were still awake, he'd warble 'Good night, little ladee', part of some song I never got to hear the rest of. But tonight it was too late for that. He must just have glanced in, and gone, for next thing the radio came on in the bedroom.

I leaned up on my elbow. The door was still ajar, but only just, only the thinnest thread of light was visible now. My father, in the bedroom, and my mother, in the bathroom, went about their mysterious, separate, adult rituals.

And I lay weeping silently, alone with my terrible secret.

The next morning Julia was up early. Both

she and the kitchen, Habitat's finest, were extra fresh and bright when I crept down to breakfast.

Dad was having a lie in.

After that, I got to know the sounds so that I woke almost before they'd begun; as though, like an epileptic, I'd begun to recognize the vibration in the air that meant trouble.

The incidents – 'episodes' they'd be called now – were not frequent. They tended to come in a spate, two or three in the space of a week, and then there would be nothing for months. Nor were they noisy. That was the worst thing about them. It was a violence contained and controlled not just by my mother's courage, and her shame, but by my father's cunning. Much more than the thumps and bangs, my father's low, mean voice going on and on, I hated the muted scrabbling in between – the sound of Julia recovering from one blow and gathering herself for the next, protecting both her face and her most precious breakable things. Keeping up appearances.

They were both brilliant at it. I suppose they had plenty of practice. My mother's pride, and her essential coldness, were Dad's greatest allies. She would – and could – have died rather than admitted publicly what was going on. And now I, though she didn't know it, was colluding with her.

Mostly, I saw nothing. I made sure of that. I would sit up in bed, gazing at the door but not wanting to shut it because then they'd know I'd heard them, just waiting for it to be over. It became one of those childhood horrors to be endured like nightmares, and first day of term, and being picked on by other kids. Only this particular horror had to be suffered in silence, and alone.

These days when I read of abused children feeling guilty, I can understand it. I may not have been abused myself, but I was crushed by guilt that I was unable to protect my mother, or restrain my father, or make everything all right. And everything was further complicated because I loved my father the most.

About a year after I first became aware of what was going on, I did see something. Not much, but enough that decades later the image is still shockingly bright and clear on my mental retina.

It was the morning after one of the episodes, and as usual I had come down to a spotless kitchen and a cooked breakfast.

Julia was in her scarlet satin happy coat and baggy black trousers – it was a non-work day – but she was still fully coiffed and made up.

I didn't feel well – it had nothing to do with what had gone on in the night, I was hot and shivery and my legs ached. When I told Julia, she placed a hand on my forehead, firmly but briefly, and pronounced it nothing serious.

'You'll be fine when you get there. You can have an early night tonight.'

My eyes filled with tears. It was all too much. Julia patted my shoulder, she must have been dying to get me out of the house.

'Cheer up darling. It's not RE today is it?' I hated RE not because of the subject but because of the teacher; a fat, angry woman with bad breath and a temper to match.

I shook my head. Julia sighed. She shared the school run, and today it was the turn of one of the other mothers, Sally Marker. I was always ready, with everything I needed and my homework done. Today was no exception. When the horn sounded, Julia opened the door and ushered me gently forth. I got as far as the car and burst into tears. Sally was a breezy, easygoing, good-hearted woman. She leapt out at once and put her arm round me.

'What's up, Fee? Mm? Sweetie? This isn't like you.'

'She doesn't feel well,' called Julia. 'She'll be okay when she gets there.'

'I'm not so sure about that...' Sally felt my face rather more solicitously than my mother had done. 'You are hot, aren't you?'

I nodded. I knew I was letting the side down, but I was past caring. I wanted to be back in my bed, tucked up cosy with a glass of lime juice and the portable TV. As I stood there sobbing Julia came and joined us – I could smell her perfume, and feel her hand on my neck, but I didn't look up. It must have been horribly embarrassing – not to say unprecedented – for her to be cast in the role of the uncaring parent packing their sick child off to school, but she played it well, like the experienced dissembler she was. I heard her say, in a musing voice: 'Oh dear, did I get this wrong?'

'I don't know, these things can be so hard to judge. She really does seem a bit rocky,' said Sally. 'I hate to interfere, but – what do you think?'

'Maybe...' There was a muted discussion over my head, resulting in my being led back to the house. The relief was so intense it outweighed my shame.

'Okay,' said my mother as she closed the door after us. 'Up you go and jump into bed. I'll come and take your temperature in a minute, see how long you're likely to survive.'

There was no doubt she was irritated and upset, and with good reason, but presented with a *fait accompli* her administration was faultless, as I knew it would be. There was no kiss, no cuddle, no comforting words – but when she came into the bedroom she made everything neat and soothing. The lime juice had ice in it, she put away my school clothes, produced a clean Disney T-shirt and a fresh extra pillow, and placed her own bedroom radio-cassette player (I wasn't due one till my next birthday) on the bedside table.

'Don't worry,' she said, popping the thermometer in my mouth. 'I've got spare batteries.'

My temperature was a hundred and one. 'Looks like you win,' she said, without smiling. She held out two junior paracetamol in the palm of her hand and I swallowed them dutifully.

'What about a book? Tintin if you like.' This was a huge concession, but I shook my head. 'Story tape?'

'No thanks.'

'Right then.' She patted the edge of the bed, not me, and stood up. 'I'll leave you to it. Give a shout if you need anything, I'll be around.'

She always spoke to me – the tone if not the words – as if I were an adult. That was why she wanted us to call her by her name. She was, then anyway, the most naturally unmaternal woman I've ever known.

She left the room, leaving the door ajar as she did at night, and went downstairs. I dozed, at first hot and aching and then, as the pills took effect, cooler and slightly sweaty. Dad didn't have to be at the office of *London Lights* till ten, and about half an hour later I heard him emerge, with his radio, and go into the bathroom. It strikes me now how bizarre it was that Julia, having been subjected to what he handed out, still went to bed with him. What happened in there? Did he apologize? Kiss it better? Did they have sex? You hear of relationships where a degree of violence is the natural precursor to sex, but it was so hard to believe.

At any rate, on that morning I did not worry. There was never any trouble the day after – the tension had been relieved, the deed was done, all was everyday and peaceful. It was the measure of my silent complicity in the situation that I shared in its moods and its changing temperature.

When my father came out of the bathroom I heard him pause, and then the radio was switched off and he opened the bedroom door. He was wearing his dark-blue towelling dressing gown and his hair was wet. There was a spot of shaving cream at the corner of his mouth.

'Hallo there – what's up?'

'I don't feel well.'

'Poor old Fifi.' He came over and gave me a kiss, smoothing my hair as he did so. He smelt sweet and his new-shaven cheek was soft. 'What a bugger. Still, day in bed, just the thing.'

'Yes,' I agreed fervently.

'Got everything you want?'

'Yes thanks.' I glanced at his hands – they were unmarked.

'Mum's at home today anyway, isn't she?' The only time I ever heard the word 'Mum' applied to Julia was from his lips.

'Yes.'

'All right for some. I'm off to earn a living.'

I didn't reply. Weirdly, I was tongue-tied with embarrassment for him. It was so awful to know what he did, to have heard him doing it only a few hours ago, and now to have him here being his droll, likeable everyday self. The knowledge bestowed on me a power that I didn't want.

'I'm going to a boring party this evening,' he said, 'so I'll be back late. I hope you're much better in the morning.' He turned in the doorway and smiled a conspirator's smile. 'But not so much better that you have to go to school, of course.'

I smiled back weakly. I was sure he wouldn't find the party boring. I hated myself for my inability to hate him. It seemed I was being a traitor to everyone, even myself.

Shortly after that he left, calling 'Bye Fifi!' as he jogged down the stairs. During the next five minutes perfectly normal morning conversation and sounds drifted up from the kitchen, and then the front door closed behind him. Before dozing off I entertained the desperate, crazed hope that I'd got it all wrong.

I woke feeling hot again, and with my bladder full of the half pint of lime juice I'd drunk. I staggered groggily out of bed and opened the door – Julia must have closed it so as not to disturb me. There were two lavatories upstairs – one my parents had put in when they refitted the bathroom, and the original, separate one which had no radiator and was always cold. I headed for the warm bathroom. This took me past my parents' bedroom. The door was open about a foot – enough for me to see the mirrored door of Julia's walk-in wardrobe, and her reflection in it.

I froze. She was standing in front of her dressing table, with no clothes on. But the shock of her nakedness was utterly eclipsed by the wound on the side of her ribs, just below the breast – a wound she was dressing with flinching, excruciating care, using cotton wool and the contents of a bottle that stood open on the dressing table. It took no more than a couple of seconds for me to take in the puffy, scarlet flesh, the raw purplish edges standing proud where the skin had cracked, the scattering of blotches over her waist and thigh. I had never seen my mother look vulnerable, I didn't even know the word, but there was something inexpressibly sad about her quiet, lonely concentration. She was covering up, and if she caught me watching her it would be as if I, personally, had reopened the wound with my bare hands.

Nauseous with horror and misery I crept back into my room, closed the door, and slid beneath the duvet. Tears sparked behind my eyelids but my face felt rigid, afraid to move. If there had been any hope, however pathetically misplaced, it was gone now.

Three

When they separated, you'd think I'd have been relieved, but I wasn't. I was terribly cut up. The remorse was awful – I took it all on board, and felt that maybe if I'd been able to do something, or told someone, things might have been different. Nobody else knew, I was sure of that. They were regarded with amused and slightly baffled affection by their friends – they were an odd couple, but no-one could believe they were splitting up, so there was the double discomfort of being the sole carrier of the secret. I could not even be said to have been complicit, because my parents themselves were unaware of my burden.

But who would I have told? And what could they have done that would not have involved the most appalling humiliation – for all of us, but especially for my mother? I could never, never, have told Julia, any more than I could have let on I'd seen her that morning, applying witch hazel to her injuries. We were all trapped, but separately – cut off from each other and from any hope of comfort.

It was a terrible burden for a child to bear. It would have destroyed me if Hannah had to go through anything like that. But one thing it taught me was that it wouldn't destroy *her*. Children are astonishingly stoical and accepting. When Dad left, Julia and I moved out to the suburbs, to leafy Winchmore Hill, and she got a new job as secretary to a firm of solicitors. She was so smart and good-looking, she must have had admirers, but if she did I wasn't aware of it. To begin with Dad visited regularly, and it was nice to see him. He was always on his best behaviour and sometimes all three of us would go out together – to the pictures, or the park, or to have a pizza – as though we were still a family. But the visits became less and less frequent over the years and when they petered out altogether I accepted that, too. I'd trained myself not to think about the past, or speculate about the future. The habit of non-intrusion had become thoroughly ingrained.

I have no idea whether Julia and Miles kept in touch after that. As far as I was concerned my father simply grew fainter, and dissolved. 'Slow fade' they'd call it in a film. He must have been helping out financially because after we moved I was sent to St Faith's, a twee local private school with a blue, white and grey uniform. I hated the school, particularly the secondary phase, and my teenage years marked the temporary breakdown of my relationship with my mother.

So much had depended on us both playing our parts, but when I hit thirteen I could no longer be bothered. All that was history. The hormones kicked in, boys, fashion and music filled, or at least covered, the black hole of guilt and unhappiness. We'd never been demonstrative with each other. Her way of showing affection was through the efficient administration of domestic life, and now I found all that irritating beyond belief. Little ingrate that I was, I decided that her control and efficiency was for her benefit, not mine, and she could stuff it.

I wasn't just a rebel, I was a nightmare. When I got pregnant the first time at the age of seventeen it was no surprise to anyone except me. What had I thought, that I led a charmed life? I miscarried very early on, and perhaps it was just as well. The day I lost it I didn't shed a single tear, but went out in the evening and got completely off my face. It happened again a year later, and this time I didn't tell Julia, and swung a termination on the NHS. I managed to persuade them that I was an unfit parent – not a hard task. In both cases the boys concerned – I won't call them 'fathers' – cared jack shit about me or the baby, so that wasn't an issue. When I left the hospital I had a prescription for the pill in my pocket.

I left school with nothing to show for it, shacked up with a better-qualified friend and worked in shops and bars. For more than ten years I only saw Julia if I wanted something. To her eternal credit she never criticized (she probably thought it was her fault), and always baled me out if she could. But gradually, over the years, almost without my noticing, I was calming down. I met Dean, the owner of the Slice of Life sandwich bar. He was younger than me, handsome, hardworking and solvent. Most of all, he was crazy about me. We moved in together. I wanted to keep my end up and make him proud of me, so I took a computer course in the evenings. I should have been on my way, but not long after that I had a slip up with the pill and fell pregnant again. To tell the truth I wasn't sure what I thought about it, but when I told Dean he was beside himself, so I decided to go ahead.

It was a good time. I was in my late twenties, and earning. I had a bloke, a flat and a baby on the way. I decided on the spur of the moment to look up Julia and show her that I had not gone to the dogs as she'd anticipated. Not for her satisfaction, you understand, but for my own.

But if I'd changed, she hadn't. She behaved as if she'd only seen me the day before, and heard my news with her usual coolness and containment. In the space of a few minutes my emotional glass went from half full to half empty. In her eyes I was still a ne'er do well, a single mother with no qualifications and no prospects. She didn't actually ask me how I thought I was going to manage. What she said was: 'What if it doesn't work out with you and the father?' Pointing out, of course, that I was dependent on Dean. If ever there was a moment when I was going to let it all out about the past, that was it. But somehow, I contained myself, and my restraint made me feel superior.

Anyway, we were back in contact and the forthcoming baby gave Julia a project, especially with my being so useless. I was sure that her new acquaintances – she didn't have any close friends – had been told about me, and probably admired her for being such a brick, coping with her troubled, prodigal daughter, and the grandchild on the way. I decided to let her get on with it. If she wanted to buy baby stuff, and knit, that suited both of us.

The day Hannah was born, right on time, I at last discovered something for which I had a natural aptitude: first time out, I gave birth like a peasant. Two and a half hours, no pain relief and no stitches – textbook stuff according to the hospital midwife.

Dean decided not to be there. In spite of his enthusiasm, he turned out to be squeamish, one of those blokes who go the old-fashioned route, hovering in the corridor with a cup of plastic coffee and a furrowed brow. Next thing you know he was being ushered in to find us propped up on the pillows, hair combed and everything in place, looking sweetly radiant ... From time to time I would wonder if he'd had any children since and whether he'd got the impression it was always going to be that quick and easy. If so, I pitied the other women.

Anyway, Hannah and I were stars not just for a day, but for oh, about six weeks? Then the novelty wore off, and the sleepless, sexless nights began to bite, and Dean turned ugly. Good phrase that, 'turned ugly'– because in his case it was almost literally true. He was so good-looking, but that began to change, along with his mood. Out went the sunny charm and ready smile, the openness and the sense of humour, to be replaced by a tight mouth and a cold-eyed scowl.

Even so, I thought it was only a phase, that it would wear off as Hannah grew up and became her Daddy's girl. I based this on how Dad had been with me – the jokes and kisses and the calling me 'Fifi'. I didn't think of Dad the bully and wife-beater. So it came as a shock when one evening Dean shouted at us. He came back from the sandwich bar and things were in a mess, and I was half asleep breastfeeding Hannah in front of the telly, and he went berserk. He began 'tidying up', throwing things into boxes and baskets, or just plain throwing things, crashing the baby buggy into the wall, yelling all the time about did I think I was the first woman in the world to have a baby, and was I never going to do a fucking useful thing ever again? Hannah's little arms flew up in shock at the first shout, and then she began screaming, and didn't stop till long after Dean had slammed out of the house. Looking back I'm sure it was nothing out of the ordinary, only an attention-seeking tantrum, a 'Me, me, me!' in the face of too much domesticity – a scene that was probably being played out in thousands of neo-natal households all over the country. But suddenly the past, which had been biding its time, lying in wait for just such a moment, reared up in front of me, black and hideous and terrifying.

It only took three such outbursts, during which it must be said Dean didn't come close to laying a finger on either of us, and I was out of there. I packed up and went, shamelessly, home to Julia. It was characteristic of her that she didn't crow. She didn't need to: I had come back and that spoke for itself. Over the next few weeks she fended Dean off, though I think that in fact she had quite got to like him, and when I was ready to see him again we looked at each other and wondered what on earth we'd been thinking of. We forgave each other for the mistake but he, like Dad, performed another slow fade, and it was me who was left holding the baby.

I shan't dwell on the time between then and now. I had a bumpy ride, richly deserved, some might say. But somehow or other, with my mother's assistance, I got by, got a job, found myself a rented 'studio flat' – estate agent speak for glorified bedsit – in Stoke Newington, and moved on. I was wary of men, but I did go out with a few blokes. I was lucky that Hannah was a good baby and toddler, very little trouble to me, my mother, or the childminder where she went once I was working as a secretary at the vets.

One odd thing happened while she was at the childminder's – only a small incident, but it sticks in my mind, because it was the first in a series which culminated in my experiences at Arbury Road. The childminder, Gloria, had four charges, but there was only one day, Wednesday, when they were all there together, and on that day her own daughter, Christine, helped out.

On Wednesdays we had a four p.m. surgery and I was often held up with all the people bringing Tiddles or Pongo in after work. I always rang Gloria to say if I was going to be late – she was fine with it as long as she knew

44

where I was. On this occasion it had been hectic and I didn't arrive till gone six thirty. It was late January, with a fine, spiteful sleet pricking the darkness. Christine had left and Gloria was out in the kitchen loading the washing machine, with Hannah, then aged eighteen months, watching her from the high chair with a slice of peanut butter toast in her fist.

'Don't panic, Mum,' said Gloria, who often spoke, as it were, with Hannah's voice. 'We're right as rain. Coffee?'

I kissed Hannah's warm, sticky cheek and pulled up a chair next to her. She paid me no never-mind, she was never a clingy child.

'Lots of sick animals today?'

'Too many.'

'Time of year I expect.'

'Could be.'

'Anything had to be put down?'

'Not this time, no.'

'That's good. I couldn't do that.'

It was our usual undemanding type of exchange, but it was restful, just as it was restful sitting in Gloria's cluttered kitchen with the sleet pattering on the steamed-up window, and the burble of the washing machine competing with Soppy FM. When I'd finished my coffee it was an effort to get up and prepare Hannah for the trip home, about twenty minutes on foot or less if we coincided with the bus at the bus stop. Hannah was even less keen than me, and put up a bit of a fight until Gloria stuck a finger of Kit-Kat in her hand. I sometimes wondered how often during her long day Gloria resorted to bribery, but I always wound up telling myself it didn't matter. Gloria was kind, trustworthy, and genuinely loved children; a little spoiling and tooth-decay was a small price to pay.

The phone rang just as we were ready and I left Gloria to answer it and went into the narrow hallway to put Hannah in her buggy. The door of the living room, where the children spent most of the day, was open. The room was warm and brightly lit and still littered with toys. There was a large old-fashioned wooden playpen opposite the door and to my surprise there was a baby in it, standing holding on to the bars. She – I could tell it was a girl in spite of the ubiquitous dungarees – was about a year old, with dark curly hair and bright, penetrating dark eyes. She was beautiful, she could have stepped out of one of those sentimental Victorian paintings which one dismisses as hopelessly idealized.

'Hallo,' I said, in that stupid way you talk to babies, 'who are you?'

In return I was treated to a fierce, implacable stare. It struck me as strange that she was still in here, in the playpen, while Gloria and I had been in the kitchen chatting and drinking coffee. On the other hand she seemed perfectly happy and placid and I could hear Gloria's voice, still on the phone – she would doubtless come through and see to her charge when she'd finished.

Hannah began to wriggle and I felt the Kit-Kat being dragged through my hair. The baby sank down to the ground, still gazing at me through the bars. I waggled my fingers.

'Bye-bye.'

The next day when I dropped Hannah off, I said to Gloria: 'What a beautiful baby that is – the one who was still there when we left.' I looked round. 'Is she here today?'

'Sorry?' Gloria was in early-morning harassed mode, not really concentrating. 'Doesn't look like it, no.'

And in fact I didn't see the baby again. Not there, anyway.

Four

They were hard, those years in Stoke Newington. Not much money, hard work, and what play there was was with Hannah. I spent great, yawning tracts of time at weekends wandering in parks and sitting in playgrounds. At home I wasn't one of those *Sesame Street* mothers, I was never any good at creative activities, I always wound up getting irritable. But I liked reading aloud, we did lots of that, and Hannah learned to read young; she'd always get into bed happily with a book, and then sleep like a top.

In that respect she went on being easy – because there was just her and me she was grown-up for her age, adaptable and savvy and able to hold her own in adult company. But she had her father's temper and my stubborn, rebellious streak and we often clashed. On two occasions the neighbours complained about our shouting matches. I'm sure they thought I was a terrible mother. But the thing was, we had these volcanic rows, both of us yelling and red-faced, and then we got over it. Like stags locking horns we didn't want or intend to do any real damage. We only had each other, so we were going to stick together.

When she started school, Hannah's precocity was a disadvantage. The local primary was fine, but tough. She was mouthy and confident – a bit too ready to speak up. That made her unpopular with some of her teachers and classmates. Fortunately, she was resilient, and gradually, the hard way, she learned the value of give and take and made a few friends, so she was no longer a social pariah.

We saw Julia about once a month. She and Hannah got on so well, it was hard not to feel jealous. I suppose Julia had looked after Hannah quite a bit as a baby, they had formed a relationship which was quite different to the one I'd had with my mother at that age. And thank God for it, I reminded myself – that toxic mixture of fear, and guilt and shame and suspicion, I wouldn't have wished it on my worst enemy, let alone my growing daughter.

Dean was out of the picture. I was abso-lutely determined not to ask for a penny from him, and that paid off, for a while, because he was a decent bloke and his donations to the cause had been generous, if irregular. I had preferred to rely on his good nature than be in the nagging but beholden state which was the alternative. This way I had stayed independent, and whatever he gave he gave freely. But not long after Hannah started school the contributions had stopped and I heard via a mutual acquaintance that he'd gone to the States.

We soldiered on in Stoke Newington, but desperately needed more space, and as soon as I joined Small World Travel, who paid better than the vet, I began looking around for another flat. Buying was out of the question, but I reckoned if I could find somewhere that wasn't much more expensive I could begin saving for a down payment.

Things began to look up again. My boss Anita became a good friend, and Kenny was all right too in his geeky way. I liked the students and the work was fun. We went out on a Saturday and looked at places to let. Hannah liked doing this – in fact she liked everywhere we saw. Instant gratification was the name of the game. 'Can we have this one? Can we live here?' she'd ask every time.

I may not have been the most educational

or improving of parents, but I enjoyed these outings, and on the way back we'd sometimes drop off at the Natural History or Science Museum, have a look round and tea in the café. It was like walking a dog: I'd proceed at a measured pace and Hannah would orbit me at speed, pointing out this and that, moving on before I'd got there, paying no attention to my skimpy dissertations on the exhibits. But it gave me the sense of doing some good, and she enjoyed it, so we were both happy.

On the day we'd been to see the flat in Arbury Road, we went to the Foundling Museum in Coram Fields. It wasn't far from Small World Travel, and I'd been promising myself a visit for some time.

'*What* are we going to see?' enquired Hannah suspiciously for the umpteenth time. I explained about Coram the philanthropist, and the children who would have had no home but for him. She gazed out of the window of the bus, wearing an expression of stoicism and patience sorely tried.

In fact, she enjoyed it. The museum was small and well-presented, and the presence of a couth and welcoming café near the entrance offered the promise of compensations to come. There weren't many people there, and you'd have needed a heart of stone not to be moved by the pictures of mothers giving up their babies, and the hundreds of little tokens – lockets, buttons, coins, beads, labels – left with the children as identification in case, as sometimes happened, the mother's fortunes changed and she returned. There were some heart-rending letters written by, or for, the wretched mothers, explaining the reasons for their actions, ranging from extreme poverty to sickness and, in one case, incarceration in Newgate with every likelihood of being hanged.

Hannah was horrified, but deliciously so.

'What do you think they ate?'

'It says here, look – gruel, bread and milk, porridge ... But dinner was nice. Lots of beef.'

We were gazing at eighteenth-century handwritten ledgers in a glass case. Above the documents hung a Victorian photograph, greatly enlarged, showing a craggy-faced white-haired woman dressed in black bombazine, sitting bolt upright on a hard chair, flanked by several of her small charges, all girls, in starched pinafores. It was hard to imagine, but the woman must have been what would now be called a 'carer'. The photograph wasn't perfect, and the glass caught the light from the window behind us. I moved a little to one side and now I could see a girl I hadn't noticed before, on the left and a little separate from the others. Unlike them she wasn't wearing a pinny – maybe she'd been a new arrival at the time of the photograph. This impression was borne out by her dark hair, which was not neatly tied back like that of the rest, but hung in a luxuriant mop round her face. She can't have been more than four years old, but she was an arresting figure with her fierce black eyes and rebellious jutting jaw. She stared piercingly, accusingly, right at me, no respecter of the century that lay between us, commanding my attention. There was both anger and fear in that stare, but it was the fear that communicated itself to me.

With difficulty I dragged my gaze away, and tapped Hannah on the shoulder. 'Have you seen this picture?'

'No, what?'

'See—' I pointed, but stopped. The girl wasn't there any more.

'Who's that old lady?'

'I think she must have worked here, don't you?'

'She looks absolutely horrible.'

'She was probably okay,' I said, on auto-pilot. 'It took a long time to take a photo in those days, people had to sit still for ages so they often look rather stiff.'

Hannah lost interest and sat down on a seat where you could listen to a recording at the press of a button. I stayed where I was. The low winter light struck the glass. I moved slightly the other way. Whatever I did, the fifth girl was no longer there. Perhaps I'd seen the reflection of someone else. My heart racing, I glanced around, hoping against hope. But there was no-one else in this ground-floor gallery. And even if there had been, how could a small child have been reflected so high up...? I could make out Hannah's image in the glass now, and it was on a level with my waist. It was very, very quiet, around me at least. I seemed held in a caul of silence, beyond which I could just discern the faint recorded voice of the old lady talking into Hannah's ear, describing her time at the Foundlings Hospital in the early nineteen-hundreds.

Even my skin felt strange, a cold, damp carapace, within which the rest of me shrank like a child afraid of the dark. I had never been so sharply, sickeningly aware of the difference between body and soul. At that moment I felt as if my soul were both separate, and imperfectly protected, as if it could be simply plucked out of me. By what, I did not know, and couldn't bear to imagine.

I had to say something, to break the silence and restore me to myself, but I was almost too terrified to open my mouth. Fortunately Hannah came to my rescue, demanding that I come and look at a picture of the massed ranks of pinafored little girls doing PE in the quadrangle.

'It must have been horrible,' she said.

'Not as horrible as the alternative,' said my voice. Hearing it broke the spell, and a sweat of relief broke out on my face, my palms, in the small of my back. Suddenly I was all of a piece again, heart thumping, breath rushing, blood charging through me, all connected, functioning, whole. My surroundings, only a quiet room after all, broke over me like a wave, I was buffeted by sensation.

'Mum, your face has gone really red,' commented Hannah.

I'd heard of early-onset menopause, but this was ridiculous.

When we'd been right round that room we went upstairs to see the art collection, assembled by Hogarth to raise funds for his friend's charity. The paintings were large, and distant, there were a great many portraits of bewigged philanthropists and depictions of naval battles, a nod to Coram's nautical background. Hannah wasn't in the least interested, but on the second floor was a room dedicated to Handel – another benefactor – with chairs where one could sit and listen to music at the press of a button, and this kept her amused while I pretended to pore over old letters and sheets of music in the composer's own hand. It was all fascinating stuff but I couldn't concentrate. The face of the fifth girl was imprinted on my inner eye and came between me and whatever I looked at.

Our last port of call was the café. I had a pot of tea and Hannah an orange juice and a chocolate brownie, as a result of which she became warmly appreciative.

'It's really, really good here,' she said. 'Look, you can get pitta wraps and everything.'

'So you can.'

'A bit different to what they had when they were here,' she added virtuously. It was a remark calculated to appeal to me, but my response on this occasion was an unrewarding monosyllable.

She cast me a sidelong look, weighing up

my mood and whether it was anything to do with her. 'Can we come again?'

'You never know,' I said.

'Can we get something at the shop?'

'Okay.'

I bought Hannah a pencil, and looked at the postcards: I always bought postcards, it was something of a joke between us. There was one of the old lady with her four charges.

'No, not that one,' said Hannah, 'not that horrible old lady. This, get this!'

So I left with a sentimental Edwardian painting of an affecting reunion between a mother and child after years of separation.

Next to the shop there was a plan of the original Foundlings Hospital, and I studied it while Hannah put on her Lisa Simpson scarf and gloves. The E-shaped building had been vast and imposing like one of the grander public schools, arranged around a quadrangle the size of a parade ground. None of it remained, but where it had stood Coram Fields was now a playing field dedicated to children – adults could only enter if accompanied by a child. It closed at dusk, and on this early spring afternoon the gate was already padlocked, but we walked around the perimeter to get the feel of how it had once been. Some of the imposing houses on the outside of the square were now university halls of residence and here and there the lighted, uncurtained windows provided *vignettes* of student life – a tattooed young man in a towel; a girl in a cloche hat and scarf, working at a desk; a dragon-shaped kite pinned up as a blind.

On the far side we paused by the main gate. I was regaining my perspective, feeling calmer. I imagined the place as it had been, and mentally paid my respects to Captain Coram and his colony of lost children.

Hannah slipped her hand in mine, a rare gesture of solidarity. Not to embarrass her, I gave it a squeeze without looking down, and walked on. She proceeded in a series of dawdles and sprints, always just behind me. Twenty yards on I had to wait at the corner of the road for her to catch up. As we cross-ed the road together between the rows of headlights like a guard of honour, I experi-enced a tremendous surge of love for my daughter.

'Thanks for keeping me company,' I said, as though she'd had a choice in the matter. 'I'm glad you liked it.'

'That's okay,' she replied. 'Can we go to

the aquarium next time? They've got sharks, Corinne says it's ace.'

I got into bed that night with the happy sense of a new chapter beginning. I was reading a gently amusing romantic novel, by one of the new lad-lit authors which made it all right. At half past eleven I turned the light out and fell asleep almost at once, warm and relaxed.

A couple of hours later I woke up, all attention, as though someone had tapped me on my shoulder. My subconscious, perhaps, because my mind had made one of those startling involuntary connections which showed that it had been working all the time, in spite of me.

Hannah had been wearing the Lisa Simpson gloves my mother had given her for Christmas, and which she could scarcely be persuaded to remove since. But the small hand that had slipped so trustingly, so confidingly, into mine by the gate of Coram Fields, had been bare, and cold.

Five

I decided not to ask Hannah if she'd taken her glove off to hold my hand that afternoon. If she had, it would embarrass her to admit it; and if she hadn't, it would do my head in. Either way it was a weird question, and chances were she wouldn't even remember. I rationalized it to my own satisfaction: children were always fiddling around with their clothes.

I determined to let it go, and over the next few weeks it seemed I'd succeeded. I was busy arranging our move to Arbury Road, packing things up, throwing things out, taking boxes and bags to the charity shop. There was another fringe benefit to all this activity – I passed my fortieth birthday without breaking stride. Julia had the sensitivity to give me a generous John Lewis token in a card that made no reference to hitting middle-age. My only regret was that the place we were moving to wasn't my own.

But I promised myself that now I would start saving for that deposit.

That first weekend in the new flat we amused ourselves, playing house. All the ordinary, everyday activities became small adventures by virtue of our different surroundings. Some familiar possessions took on a new lustre, others appeared so scruffy and well-worn that we chucked them away. On Saturday afternoon we walked to the High Road, which was well supplied with cut-price shops, and bought a selection of items ranging from a bath mat to a sieve. We visited the little street market and picked up fruit, veg and a bunch of daffodils, though I suspected that once the novelty had worn off we'd be back to the usual swift one-stop trawl of the cheapest available supermarket.

On the way back I gave in to pressure and bought a DVD of the latest Disney extravaganza in Woolworth's. By six o'clock we were ensconced on the sofa, now rendered more welcoming with my Turkish throw and cushions, eating pizza with our fingers.

'We won't be doing this every day,' I told Hannah sternly.

Sufficient unto the day was the indulgence thereof. Her eyes never left the screen.

'Whatever,' she said.

After she'd gone to bed I came back into the living room and lay down full-length on the sofa, with my head propped on a couple of cushions and my feet on the arm as I'd done the night before. Anita was right, the place was already looking better. Over the years, even our old 'studio flat' had become an extension of ourselves – not difficult you might say considering its size – and I could see that this would too, given time. The fabric of the building was beginning to accept us. I gazed round, thinking of where I might put pictures, mirrors, perhaps a side table where flowers could stand – at the moment our daffodils were in a lager glass in the centre of the gate-legged table. I had never had the money to buy much furniture, and was sick of living with other people's, but there was a lot that could be done ... My eyes passed over, then returned to the patch of damp on the party wall. Pity about that. I disliked hassle, and didn't relish the thought of negotiating with the landlord, or indeed the neighbours, about this small problem. On the other hand, the patch, though faint, looked a little larger than it had yesterday, so it wasn't going to go away of its own accord, without a fight. It was irritating. I couldn't understand why I hadn't noticed it when we first looked round, but then I'd never been strong on detail, I was a gut-reaction girl. Or perhaps it hadn't been there, and the wretched neighbour's plumbing had started playing up to coincide with our arrival.

The music centre and CDs were on the middle shelf of the bookcase; I roused myself and put on Joss Stone. Incredible that a girl more than twenty years younger than me had the voice of a woman ten years older – rich with soul, scraped by pain, sweetened by love, fermented in experience.

I didn't even read, I just lay there, wrapped up in that incredible voice. When the CD finished it was an effort to get up and go to bed. I switched off the music centre and the lamp. As I took a last look round I could still clearly see the wretched damp patch, reminding me that not everything in the garden was rosy. By tomorrow evening our honeymoon here would be over. I'd have to make a list.

Next day we set off for lunch with Anita around one o'clock. I knew from long experience that whatever time she'd invited us for there wouldn't be a whiff of her famous chilli until two thirty, so I made sure

Hannah had a full tank – early breakfast and two cereal bars at midday.

Still, Hannah loved going there. Anita and Janine lived in a house they owned in Kentish Town. It was a simple two-storey terraced house but they'd made it really nice, and homely. Janine was a human rights lawyer and made good money, and Anita was much more houseproud than she let on. On Saturdays they often took off to antique fairs and car boot sales, and bought stuff, which they renovated and used cunningly in all sorts of imaginative ways. They had an old phonograph in the corner of their sitting room, and a stuffed dog that sat next to it with its head cocked: Hannah was enchanted. In the bathroom was a 1930s plaster advertising statuette of a little girl with her hand outstretched, and they used her hand for the soap and her arm for the hand towel. They had a coal scuttle full of plants, and a fireplace full of scented candles, and the walls were thick with pictures – photographs and paintings, a lot of them portraits of unknown people.

Anita was patient as only the child-free can be, she'd spend ages discussing the pictures with Hannah, speculating on who the people were, making up stories about them.

And they were like older people in that they had drawers and chests full of 'treasures', things they'd bought in markets, and abroad, *objets trouvés*, bits and pieces. They had a seaside cottage in Walberswick, but their long-term plan was to sell both this house and the cottage and buy a big place in the country which they would do up and live in for the rest of their lives. Their focus was entirely on each other, and they genuinely relished the idea of an idyllic retirement, growing old together.

When we arrived I caught an encouraging whiff of chilli in the hall. This must have been some kind of nod to Hannah – it wasn't beyond Anita to begin cooking only when her guests were into their second glass, so all the adults would be completely off their faces by the time they reached the table. Hannah went into the kitchen to 'help' make the pudding, and I sat in the living room with Janine. It was a cool spring day, and the fire was lit, but the French window was open, flowers and flames together, which gave things the agreeable air of camping. I was a little in awe of Janine, who though only a few years older than me was pre-eminent in her field, but she had such a gentle manner and was such a good listener that she made you forget her distinction and see only her niceness. She was particularly interested in our visit to the Foundlings Museum.

'I've always wanted to go, I believe they've done wonderful things there.'

'They have.'

'Is it very moving?'

'Very. Captain Coram looks like Long John Silver in his portraits, but he must have been a saint.'

'What did your daughter make of it?' Janine always distanced herself slightly from Hannah, I suspected out of a sort of politeness, an admission that this was not her area.

'She loved it, especially the café – no, she did like it. Perhaps not as much as the Natural History Museum, but she got the idea. She responded, you know?'

'Good for you,' said Janine. I glowed. She got the idea, too – that I had taken Hannah to this place, and could take credit for eliciting the response.

I asked her, cautiously, about her work. The caution was unnecessary because her discretion and integrity were watertight and she would have never so much as touched on anything that should not be mentioned.

It turned out she had recently been involved in something of a *cause célèbre*, that of a woman who wanted to abort her pregnancy when amniocentesis had shown the foetus to be the result of a rape. Janine had been appearing for the stubborn and idealistic young doctor who had refused the referral.

'What's your opinion?' asked Janine. 'It doesn't matter, we lost. Do speak freely, you're a parent, I'd be interested to know.'

I hesitated, not through lack of certainty but from a desire to be clear.

'I'm not against termination in principle, and I can understand the woman's feelings. But that seems like revenge – a misplaced revenge.'

'We simply took the view that it was murder, pure and simple.'

I had got used to the legal 'we'. I knew Janine was not necessarily stating a personal opinion, but the view of her client which she had been paid to argue.

'I don't believe that. Not if it's early enough. I suppose it's just that I don't like the idea of the baby paying, literally, for the sins of the father.'

'Of course I speak from a position of ignorance,' said Janine, 'or at least from a lack of personal experience. But isn't that

67

always the case?'

'I don't know.'

She smiled ruefully. 'Why do you think I've managed so successfully to avoid parenthood all these years? I couldn't begin to deal with that level of responsibility.'

'Oh God!' I moaned self-mockingly, covering my face with my hands.

'I'm sorry.' She laughed. 'No, Fee, you do terribly well. I meant the responsibility we can't help, at the genetic level. All the things we pass on without meaning to, or recognizing that we do. In the literal, old-fashioned sense, I find that awesome.'

'I suppose so,' I said. 'I don't care to dwell on it.'

'Most people don't,' mused Janine. 'That's what fascinates me – the casual, unthinking courage of people who have children.'

Feeling rather uncomfortable on this territory, I dragged the subject back to where we'd started.

'At any rate, on balance I'm with your client on this one but for rather more specific reasons.'

'Good,' said Janine warmly, as though it actually made a difference to her what I thought. 'As I say, we didn't prevail, but I'm encouraged that you as a mother are with us in principle...' She shifted her attention to Hannah, who had come into the room bearing a dish of cashews.

'Thank you, Hannah. Now tell me, how do you like your new flat?'

'It's nice. It's really big, and our bedroom's got a window in the ceiling.'

'Has it?' Janine looked back to me. 'You've got a skylight? What fun, I've always wanted to lie in bed and gaze at the stars.'

'It's quite dirty, actually,' said Hannah. 'It's all covered in pigeon poo.'

'But you *can* see the stars,' I insisted. 'It was clear on our first night, and I checked.'

'Anyway,' said Janine, 'you could always get the window cleaner in.'

I didn't argue with her, though it seemed to me that the chances of finding, in our part of town, a window cleaner prepared to find a way on to a flat roof above a thirty-foot central drop were remote – even if we wanted a stranger clambering about up there.

Hannah put a handful of cashews in her mouth, and squeezed on to my chair next to me. I took the dish off her and put it on the brass table between Janine and me.

'Would you like to come and see it?' she asked.

'I would, very much. Is that an invitation?'

'Yes,' I said. 'Give us a week or two and we'll be open for business.'

We talked for a while longer about the restrictions inherent in furnished lets, and the difficulties of first-time buying in London, neither of which can ever have posed much of a problem for Janine, but about which she was nonetheless sympathetic and well-informed. Then we were summoned to lunch. The extended pre-prandial period had left me slightly pissed, and at the sight of Hannah's handwritten place-cards my cup ran over.

'And it's chilli!' Hannah announced. 'My favourite!'

'I like that child's style,' said Anita. 'Someone slip her a quid pro quo.'

We left at about six, and set out to walk as far as Hannah could manage. In fact it was me who flagged after a mile, and hailed a taxi with the extravagant flourish born of desperation.

'Are you all right?' asked Hannah. 'Are you drunk?'

'No, of course not.'

'Which?'

'I am perfectly all right, and very far from drunk,' I said, sounding like every sitcom-drunk you ever heard.

'Yeah, right,' said Hannah. But in spite of her sceptical tone I knew that with Anita's fiver in her pocket, she was a happy bunny.

When we got home we supped on tea and digestive biscuits, and both fell asleep on the sofa in front of the *Antiques Roadshow*. I woke at nine, and carried Hannah along to bed, peeling off her clothes and tucking her up while reminding myself that this had better not happen next Sunday, when it would be school – the dreaded new school – the following morning. I took the fiver out of her coat pocket, rolled it up and stuffed it through the mouth of her Shrek money box.

I longed for bed, but went back along the corridor to the kitchen to slake my post-wine thirst. The overhead bulb was only a sixty-watt, which made the narrow room dingy. As I stood there glugging down a pint of tap water I promised myself to buy a stronger one tomorrow, to brighten things up a bit. In fact, the kitchen was the dreariest part of the flat. There was something sad about its cheap, freestanding units and stained check wallpaper, the imperfectly fitted plastic floor tiles. Perhaps it just needed a spring-clean. I was no enthusiast for housework, but I could rise to a challenge.

Here was something else for us to do during the remaining week of the holiday. I gazed across the dark brick ravine into our un-curtained bedroom. My reflection gazed back, mysterious against the dim light.

In bed at last, I found that after our early evening doze I was wide awake again. All the same I didn't read but turned the lamp off and lay staring up at the skylight. The night was overcast and there was nothing to see. I reflected on my earlier conversation with Janine. I hadn't, of course, mentioned my own abortion. I sensed that such an admis-sion, apart from not being appropriate to a social occasion, would have shocked Janine, the legal 'we' notwithstanding. She had cast me in the role of one of those plucky mothers she admired so much, prepared to hurl themselves into the tumultuous un-known without so much as a backward glance.

For the first time in several days I thought of Julia. In what frame of mind had she embarked on motherhood? On having *me*, her only child? There must have been a time when she and Miles had been wholly happy and in love. She was far too smart to have married an abuser, even if she had later been too proud to leave him, so presumably I had been the product of that love. I so hoped that I had been truly wanted. My own childhood memories were unreadable in that respect, just as Julia had been. She had been an exemplary mother in every way but the one that mattered. I recalled few kisses, no hugs, no direct expressions of affection. In that regard my father had ... I would have said 'left her for dead' only the phrase was tasteless in the circumstances. He was the warm, funny, doting Dad. That was why, when I became aware of the dark side of their relationship, it had been so hard to untangle my feelings. My mother repelled sympathy and understanding. My father continued, confusingly, to be the charmer he always had been. I tried to imagine them with me, as a baby – carrying me about, pushing me in a pram, gazing at me in my cot, amusing me with toys, pacifying and comforting me when I cried, sleepless, frazzled and adoring. In this affecting scenario it was once again a great deal easier to picture my father than my mother.

I tossed and turned, nudging and nosing at the past, picking at its seams, trying to open it up and see the pattern, what it was made of. But as always it resisted my attempts and eventually I tired myself out.

My last thought as I sank into a heavy small-hours sleep was that I was glad at least to have been their only child, the fruit of a happier time, and not a reminder of pain.

Six

The following weekend marked the end of the Easter holidays. For that reason it was slightly overshadowed by the prospect of my return to work and Hannah starting at her new school. I longed for the moment of separation to be over, for it to be Monday afternoon, and the worst behind us.

We went to see Julia on the Saturday. My conscience told me that I should have invited her to visit us in the new flat, but I wasn't quite ready for that. I wanted to keep this part of my life separate for a while, so Hannah and I took the bus up to Winchmore Hill.

Naturally Julia had been to considerable trouble. The reason she didn't care for spontaneity was because she liked to get things right. She'd done a roast chicken – Hannah's other favourite – and bought Hannah a purple hooded top, and me a lace-edged provençal linen tablecloth and napkins.

'It's a housewarming present,' she explained. 'I thought you might like something elegant that you wouldn't buy yourself. And they are machine washable, I checked.'

'They're beautiful,' I said truthfully. 'You must come down soon and help us christen them. And the lovely wine glasses,' I added – I'd spent the John Lewis token on a set of elegant Danish goblets.

'When you're ready, plenty of time.'

She looked great as always, much less than her sixty-four years, in jeans and a cream polo shirt, with simple gold earrings and bracelet. She wasn't a beauty, but she made up for it with attention to detail and intensive maintenance. I don't think I ever saw my mother with chipped nail polish, bad hair or a mark on her clothes. I was in awe of the effort she put in, and the courage that effort must have taken over the years. She was a woman of steel. The other side of that was her aversion to intimacy: I had never been able to get close to her, and with the passing of the years and improvements in my own life, the possibility of closeness seemed ever more remote. We were civil and pleasant with one another, equanimity was what we aimed for in our relationship. So I was thunderstruck when, at the end of lunch, when Hannah was in front of a DVD in the other room, Julia announced: 'I saw your father the other day.'

This was such a surprise that I wasn't sure I'd heard her correctly. 'What?'

'By accident – or sheer chance if you like.'

'Dad?'

'That's right.'

'Did you speak to him?'

'Of course! We could scarcely avoid it, we bumped into each other at the garden centre.'

This prosaic setting wasn't untoward where my mother was concerned, she was a keen gardener, but I could not recall Miles ever having gone voluntarily either there, the DIY centre, or even to the supermarket. He had always been conspicuously, determinedly, out of place in what he called 'lifestyle temples'.

'He wasn't alone,' said Julia. 'He was there with his new wife.'

'I didn't know he'd remarried...' I murmured. It was a lot to take in.

'Nor me, but she seemed nice enough. Younger, of course, but not obscenely so.

Very pretty. Combat trousers and so on.'

It was so hard not to ask aloud what my mother must surely have been asking herself: *I wonder if it's happened yet – I wonder if he's hit her?* Instead, I said:

'Did he seem happy?'

'Well – you know, how could I tell? He was rather disconcerted at washing up next to me by the pelargoniums, we both were. But he looked well, and quite smart.'

'Good.' I didn't know what else to say. I could hardly admit to feeling hurt that Dad had never been in touch. I was ashamed of having any affection for him after what he'd done to Julia, but he'd never treated *me* badly, and it would have been nice to have had some signs of affection or remembrance over the years.

'He asked after you. And Hannah.'

'Oh. Right.'

'I think he'd like to make contact. But I didn't give him your address or telephone number, I thought I should see how you felt about it.'

'Thanks.'

'He gave me his card, but I've copied down the details, so you could have it if you wanted, and then the ball will be in your court.'

She had done exactly the right thing, as was only to be expected. If we had been a different kind of mother and daughter we might have embraced, and had a bit of a cry, and everything would have come out. But we weren't, and it didn't.

Just as well perhaps, because there was another bombshell on the way.

'It wasn't quite the shock it would have been a few months ago,' said Julia, 'because I'm seeing someone.'

'You are?' I tried to appear thrilled, happy, not too astonished – when what I felt was gobsmacked and deeply apprehensive. 'That's wonderful.'

My mother sipped her coffee and replaced the cup on its saucer (no mugs at the table in her house) before adding, 'We're thinking of getting married.'

'Julia!' This time there was no point in pretending; being gobsmacked was not just legitimate but obligatory. 'How come you've been keeping all this to yourself?'

'It hasn't been very long, and you've been busy.'

'You're telling me it was a whirlwind romance?'

She smiled. 'It's all been quite quick. And keep it to yourself, nothing's decided yet.'

'Fine. Of course.' I stared at my mother, trying to analyse my confused feelings. I was glad, genuinely glad, if she had found happiness. But I mistrusted her motives. I couldn't help suspecting her of expediency. Then again, did that matter? If anyone was entitled to make a careful, calculated, self-interested choice it was her, after all she'd been through, and the ensuing loneliness.

'Tell me about him,' I said.

'His name's Adrian Downes, he has his own production company making short promotional films for businesses. It's successful,' she added pointedly. 'He does extremely well.'

It was typical of her to offer up only those dull, external details in which I was least interested. A great deal of Downes's attraction for Julia clearly rested on him having done well for himself, but that wasn't what I wanted to know.

'Come on,' I said, 'what does he look like?'

'Goodness ... Pleasant, in shape for his age, glasses. He tells me he's often taken for a German when he's abroad.'

'Right.'

'Handsome, in a different way from your father – but he makes more effort, he dresses better.'

'How old is he?'

'A little bit younger than me – not enough to make a fuss about.'

'Julia! Well done you.'

'I don't know about that...' Hannah came into the room and Julia held out her hand to her. She had always been more demonstrative with her granddaughter than with me; it was an altogether safer relationship. 'How's the film?'

'Cool. Granny, have you got any of those chocolate shells?'

'I might.'

'Can I have one?'

'Please may I have one,' I corrected automatically, before Julia could. She pushed her chair back and got up.

'I think so, don't you?' She got the chocolates out of the cupboard and peeled off the cellophane; she had obviously bought them specially. 'There you are – have a couple while you're at it.'

'Thanks, Granny!' Hannah helped herself and was out of there.

'Fee?'

'No thanks.'

'I think I will. That's the trouble with chocolates, once they're open I can't resist.'

She was slim as a willow and I knew she

worked on it. Now she closed the box and pushed it over the table to me. 'You'd better take them with you, otherwise I'll eat all of them.'

That was supremely unlikely and we both knew it. It was also part of our understanding that I did not give the same priority to personal maintenance, and that my own weight wobbled unevenly around the national average.

'Okay, thanks.'

'But as I say,' she went on calmly, 'we haven't set a date, so it would be best if you didn't say anything to anyone.'

'I won't, I promise.' I gazed at her, but she was quite opaque, blandly sipping her coffee. 'Did you tell Dad?' I asked.

'Heavens above no, it wasn't the time or the place ... And anyway, he wouldn't be interested.'

'Well,' I said, 'I think it's very interesting, and congratulations!' I leaned across and pecked her on the cheek.

'Thank you.'

'I tell you who else will be interested...' I pointed in the direction of the sitting room. 'As soon as you know for sure, you must tell her, she'll be made up about it.'

'Sweet, of course – as long as she realizes it

won't be a bridesmaidy sort of wedding.'

'But you could give her some little job, surely...'

'I bet I could.'

When the DVD had finished we went for a walk. There was a municipal park near my mother's house, nothing like as nice as the great London park near us but clean, and serviceable, with a playground. Julia and I stood shoulder to shoulder and watched Hannah zoom down the slide, whirl round on the roundabout and swarm over the jungle gym with her peers.

I said: 'I suppose that means Dad's living somewhere near here.'

'Not necessarily. The garden centre's a couple of miles away and it's huge, the catchment area probably extends way out.' For the first time that day I detected an edge on her voice. She didn't want Dad to be too close, and I didn't blame her.

When we left, she gave me his card. 'There you are. Over to you.'

'What was that Granny gave you just then?' asked Hannah on the way to the tube.

'Granddad's address.'

'I've never met him.'

'Would you like to?'

'I don't mind.'

This was the literal truth, not intended to be slighting, so I pushed her a little further.

'Shall we give him a ring?'

Hannah shrugged. 'Whatever.'

In this case I knew the 'whatever' – one of the most nuanced words in the junior lexicon – indicated genuine indifference. What I was less sure of was whether the indifference was good or bad. Was it the product of a healthy emotional balance, or psychological scar tissue? How usual was it for a nine-year-old to have almost no contact with her father, and none at all with her grandfather? To have, in effect, only two family members, myself and my mother, whose relationship could at best be described as unusual?

That night after she'd gone to bed I warned myself sternly not to make Hannah a pretext for satisfying my own curiosity. Because there was no denying I *was* curious about my father. It had been almost surreal sitting there in my mother's elegant drawing room, listening to her talking about him with a kind of tolerant, patronizing fondness as if he had been any useless, erring husband who couldn't help himself. I wanted my memories confirmed, or corrected. I wanted to *know*. God knows how I imagined I was going to be granted this definitive knowledge. I could scarcely reopen relations with Dad by asking outright: Did you beat your wife? And if I did, that was like the 'Are you or have you ever been a member of a terrorist group?' on the immigration form – was he really going to hold his hands up, say yes, and declare undying remorse?

In any event, the decision whether to contact him or not had to be put on hold, because there was Hannah's first day at the new school to be negotiated. I was incredibly fortunate with my work; Anita was the most broadminded and sympathetic employer imaginable, and had agreed, no, insisted, that for the first week I could get in half an hour late and leave half an hour early so Hannah wouldn't have to be left at the pre- and after-school club right away.

Regent Road was C of E affiliated, which showed my ambivalence towards these things. I'd never had any time for organized religion, but I sensed that it gave a school a certain ethos – call it safety, order, kindness, whatever you like – and I sought that for my daughter. Plus the head, Maurice Jenkins, was the genial primary head from central casting, a not-too-woolly liberal who plainly not only liked children but was liked equally by them. On both the occasions I'd been there, once on my own and once with Hannah, the atmosphere had been warm, welcoming and productive, a place where learning was no hardship and teaching ... Well, I couldn't have done it, but more power to those whose vocation it was.

It was still awful leaving her. The cold, wet morning didn't help but at least the rain meant Hannah wouldn't notice the odd tear. She herself was grim and tight-lipped. I was proud of her. Dean, damn him, would have been proud of her. I felt a surge of implacable cold fury towards my daughter's absent father. Talk about a negative experience of fatherhood, she was going to grow up thinking all men buggered off the minute they had children; or, worse, would see that they didn't and assume that her own situation was all her fault.

She went off without a backward glance. But I was back there, first mother at the gate, at three p.m. It was still raining. A man in a suit joined me and when the rain found another gear we moved into the covered area at the side of the playground.

'No improvement in the parking,' he remarked affably. 'I feel like a marked man coming on my own in the urban tractor.'

'I don't own a car,' I said, 'so I don't know.

Is it a problem?'

'Oh, frightful. Tempers run high. Nothing I can do, when it's my turn I have to drive and there's no-one to share with. But in your case,' he smiled, 'your conscience is crystal clear.'

'Only by default. I'd kill for a car.'

He smiled. 'You know that. Now I know that, too. But no-one else does, so keep schtum and take the credit.' He held out his hand. 'Mark Proctor, by the way.'

'Fiona Wade.' I used my mother's maiden name.

'Hallo. You'll have to excuse me if we've met before, but I'm only here from time to time. Divorced-dad syndrome.'

'Right. No, we haven't. This is my first day. Our first day.'

'Son? Daughter?'

'Hannah – she's nine, she's with Mrs Jaynes.'

'There you go, Reuben's in that year too.'

We smiled slightly vacantly at each other, pleased at this small coincidence but not sure what it proved. Other parents were beginning to arrive. A woman came up to Mark Proctor and began talking about some event unconnected with school. I could tell that he was bait – a single man in his mid-thirties with all his own hair and teeth and a Porsche Cayenne. Given the opportunity to observe unobserved, I noticed that his lived-in looking suit was expensive and he had customized it with a nice plaited b lt. His hair was well cut but left just long enough to show that it was curly. After a minute he tapped my arm and introduced me to the other woman.

'By the way, this is Fiona Wade, her daughter just started today. Fiona, this is Gilly Clarkson.'

'Fee,' I said. 'Hallo Gilly.'

'Hallo!' Her eyebrows shot up as she pumped my hand, she was one of those women bristling with a generalized enthusiasm that latched on to whatever was nearest. 'Great, welcome, what year?'

'Mrs Jaynes,' I said.

'Oh, Marie's so *lovely*,' groaned Gilly in an ecstasy of approbation. 'She gave my two such a marvellous grounding!'

'Gilly has twins,' explained Mark, 'among the shining ones in year six.'

'Wow,' I said. As the children began to pour forth from the double doors and I scanned the sea of faces for Hannah's, I realized that it was at least as hard, and a great deal more complicated, being a new parent than a new pupil.

Hannah washed up by my side, looking composed but slightly grumpy and carrying a blue cardboard folder.

'Hallo, you,' I said. 'How was your day?'

'All right.'

She didn't even look at me, her eyes were casting about suspiciously for someone else. Mark Proctor greeted his son; a boy of about Hannah's age, but shorter and chunkier, with an extremely cool Diesel parka.

'Okay,' said Proctor. 'I'd better go before I get moved on with menaces. Bye, nice to meet you. Reuben, move it—'

Hannah glared after them. 'I hate that boy,' she said.

'Do you? Why's that?'

'He's really, really horrible and he shows off.'

'Never mind,' I said with a sinking heart. 'Were the others nice?'

'Suna and Meriel are nice.'

'Good. And the teacher, Mrs Jaynes, did you like her?'

'She's okay.'

'So all in all,' I said, taking her hand and heading for the crossing. 'Not a bad day.'

She didn't reply. She was reserving judgement, not about to give me the satisfaction of an unqualified 'yes'. But that was fine. A pity about Reuben Proctor, but all things considered we were over the first hurdle.

At home Hannah showed me the contents of her folder. There was a letter from Mrs Jaynes saying that she was always available to parents, and that for their part parents were welcome both as helpers and visitors, and might like to have lunch in school every so often to see how good the food was; there was a picture Hannah had done; a reading-scheme book which I knew was way inside her capabilities; and a note of events during the summer term 'for the diary' – sports, fête and end-of-year concert. Apparently there would be a small amount of homework each week, but not till the second week of term.

I rang my mother as instructed to tell her all was well, and passed the handset to Hannah. Her answers were monosyllabic. When I got the handset back, Julia said: 'Not very communicative, but I expect she's tired.'

'I think so.'

'All well, as far as you know?'

'Absolutely.'

'I realize you can't speak freely. Why don't you ring again at the end of the week and give me an update?'

'We will.'

That evening Hannah went through various phases; the first of slightly excitable relief, the second of contentment, the third of grumpy tiredness and then, at bedtime, a last-minute resurgence of tension about the next day.

'I don't want to go.'

'Oh, sweetie...' I sat down on the bed. 'I bet you don't. But that's only first day-itis. Don't think about it now, it'll seem different in the morning.'

'It won't.'

For the second time that day, my heart sank. 'You didn't have any real problems, did you?'

She put her arms over her face, but I could see her mouth, with the lips pressed together. I loved her so much, and was such a useless parent, I could have wept for both of us. I rubbed her arm.

'Mm?'

She shook her head, indicating that she didn't want to tell me rather than that there weren't any problems.

'It won't seem so big once you've said it,' I intoned.

She muttered something and rolled over,

away from me. I put my head down near hers.

'Sorry sweetie? What was that?'

'I hate Reuben…'

'What does he do?'

'He called me a boff.'

'Maybe he's a thicko,' I suggested spiritedly. She ignored this. 'Take no notice,' I added, knowing that the soundness of this advice was completely inaccessible to a nine year old.

'I can't help it. He goes on and on. And about my shoes.'

'Your *shoes*?'

'Can I have trainers with laces?'

'Well, I don't see why—'

'I mean can we get some on the way tomorrow?'

'There won't be a shoe shop open at that time.'

This was greeted by a short silence, full to bursting with Hannah's resentment and unhappiness.

'We'll see,' I said weakly. Something occurred to me. 'What about—' I cudgelled my brains till they yielded up a name – 'Suna? What sort of shoes does she have?'

'I don't know.'

'Your other friend, then—'

'I haven't got another friend.'

'Yes you have, you told me, you said two names – you said they were nice. Mary?'

'Meriel.'

'That's it. What about her?'

Hannah shook her head, dumb with misery. I saw that it mattered diddly-squat what Suna and Meriel wore – my daughter was being picked on by the vile Reuben, and he had got to her. It was this wretched boy, not her shoes, that was the problem.

'Don't worry,' I said firmly, planting a kiss on her cheek. 'I bet we've got something else you can wear for just one day, we'll see what we can find.'

Fortunately, she didn't have the energy to fret for long. Unlike me – I fretted for hours. The only other footwear Hannah possessed were wellies, and a pair of wildly unsuitable pink suede slip-ons.

I was upset, frustrated and outraged. All this over a couple of strips of Velcro! There was a twenty-four-hour supermarket a quarter of a mile away which had own-brand clothes and shoes, but it might have been Outer Mongolia for all the chance I had of getting there. I knew no-one else in the building, or even close enough to call up and ask to babysit for an hour. I was subject to circumstantial pin-down. I railed against the absent Dean, and bloody Dad, snug with his new wife and deleted conscience. Hannah had cried herself to sleep and these two – these two *bastards* knew nothing about it and cared less.

In a fine fury I dug out the card Julia had given me, and dialled the number. A woman's voice answered almost at once. I asked to speak to Miles.

'I'll get him – who is that, please?'

'His daughter.'

'Oh...! Fiona?' I didn't answer. 'Hallo. Yes of course, hang on.'

There was a muffled silence while she prepared Miles for his second shock in a matter of days. Good! I sincerely hoped he was bricking himself, but when he came on the line he sounded teasing and sunny as ever.

'Fee! Is it really you?'

No, I wanted to say: it's Nemesis. The desire to confront him with everything, to dump him squarely in the shit, was strong, but that wouldn't have helped Hannah, and right now she was my priority.

'You ought to see your granddaughter,' I said.

'Of course I should!' He made it sound as if I'd extended an invitation rather than dished out an order. 'I really want to. Life is so good at—'

'When?' I snapped.

'Um, I don't know, what do you—'

'Next weekend?'

'Hang on.' There was more muffling. I really hoped they had an arrangement and that he was going to feel obliged to change it.

Fat chance. 'Fee, I'm so sorry, we're due to be away from Saturday for a couple of weeks. Why don't you give me your number and I'll give a bell before we go with a place and time.'

The arrogance of it – the sheer, breathtaking, selfish arrogance! Through a red mist I saw my mother, standing by her dressing table wincing as she dabbed at her wounds.

'No,' I said through gritted teeth. 'Don't bother. We don't have a car. I'll call you.'

'Fee—'

'We'll see you then. Perhaps. Whenever.' I hung up. There were spots in front of my eyes. I was fizzing, boiling, with rage and adrenalin.

Fucking Dad, fucking Reuben, fucking Velcro!

The next morning we left early, went to the

supermarket and bought some blue and white trainers with laces which could be tucked in (not tied) in the approved manner. I justified the expense by telling myself that Hannah could wear the old, uncool trainers around the house, but I knew she wouldn't. When we got to school, I considered going in and having a word with Mrs Jaynes, but decided on balance that to come across as fussy and over-protective this early in the term would be unhelpful.

I saw Reuben being dropped off by his father, jumping out of the Cayenne and steaming into the playground like the little thug he was. A pity, because Mark Proctor himself had seemed a perfectly nice man.

At work, Anita asked me how things were going. I told her I'd tell her on Friday. She said: 'Good as that, huh?'

No flies on Anita.

Seven

Things settled down, gradually. It was perfectly obvious Hannah was never going to like Reuben Proctor, but her dislike of him became part of the fabric of everyday school life – institutionalized, if you like, rather than a big issue. I discovered that he was regarded generally as a bit of a trouble-maker, so at least it wasn't just us. I picked up on this during the first week at the school gate, before Hannah started after-school club. Meriel's mother, Olwyn, who was the soul of good sense and a thoroughly nice woman, simply raised her eyes to heaven when I mentioned our spot of difficulty.

'Join the club...!'

'What, you too?'

'Initially, oh awful. I'm sure he's a nice lad really, but a chronic attention-seeker. If you can somehow persuade Hannah not to react, he'll be forced to get his kicks elsewhere.'

This accorded with my view, so I passed on the information to Hannah and repeated my earlier advice. By the end of the second week I was able to tell Anita with reasonable confidence, that things were going fine.

I saw Mark Proctor again the following Friday when I collected Hannah at the regulation time. This time he was wearing jeans and a fleece rather than the business suit.

'Afternoon off,' he said, as if an explanation were needed. 'I'm glad we've finally got spring, we're driving up to Derbyshire to stay with friends for the weekend.'

I wondered if the friends had kids and if they knew what they were taking on. Still, Mark got a whole clutch of brownie points from me, just for being there. And for greeting his son with obvious, if harassed, affection when he rocketed out of the door. He was a nice man.

With Hannah settled at school, work picked up, and I didn't have as much time or energy, as I would have liked, to do things to the flat. But I was sufficiently worried about the damp in the living room to go and knock on the neighbours' door. They were medical students, also tenants, living in some chaos, but they had no damp that they knew of, and no plumbing problems that might have accounted for it. They showed me the wall on their side to prove it, and there was no doubt it was bone dry. I rang the landlord's agent from work one lunchtime.

'Are you sure?' asked the young woman. 'The previous tenant never reported any damp, and there was certainly none there when we inspected it after he left.'

'Well there is now,' I said, 'definitely. On the party wall in the living room. And it's getting bigger.'

'Have you spoken to the people on that side?'

'Yes. They've got no damp. They showed me.'

'What about upstairs?' she asked.

'It couldn't be from there – it's halfway down the wall, at about head height.'

'Pipes can be funny old things,' she said playfully.

'Look,' I said, 'it's worrying me. Do you think you could possibly come and take a look, just to set my mind at rest?'

She agreed to send someone round that evening, between eight and ten. Annoyingly, when I got home with Hannah at six, the patch seemed fainter and smaller. I went over and put my hand on the wall. It didn't feel at all damp, and at this range the patch was scarcely visible. Typical. Just as the symptoms of terminal illness diminished the moment one walked through the surgery door, there would be nothing to see when the agent's plumber got here.

He arrived just as Hannah had got into bed, so of course she got straight out again to watch. He was understandably sceptical.

'I know this flat, and there's no reason for any damp. Sound as a bell, these houses. Built to last.'

'I agree, but there's definitely something going on.'

'Over here, you say.'

'Yes. It's not so noticeable at the moment—'

'Invisible, really.'

'It seems to come and go,' I persisted, as politely as I could manage, 'which is why I think it's connected with someone else's plumbing.'

He shook his head, eyes closed and lips pursed for greater emphasis. 'Not there it's not.' He knocked the wall with the knuckle of his forefinger. 'Sorry. Want me to take a look round while I'm here? Might as well.'

'Yes – thank you.'

He spent fifteen minutes or so running

taps, banging on pipes, peering into the airing cupboard and examining the tank, with Hannah in close attendance. At least he didn't suck up to her, but behaved as if she wasn't there apart from the odd ''Scuse me, love' when she was in his way.

'Nope.' He returned and shrugged on his denim jacket. 'All seems fine. Been well maintained, these properties. Not shoddy like some conversions.'

'Oh well,' I said, 'thanks anyway. Sorry you had a wasted journey.'

'No worries.'

The moment the door closed behind him I chased Hannah back to bed. Then I made myself a cup of tea and went back into the living room, casting an accusing glare at the perfectly clear wall.

I watched TV until about ten thirty, and then switched off and returned my mug to the kitchen, where I launched the washing machine on its long, nocturnal economy cycle. I went into the living room to turn off the lights. As I left the room I glanced back and experienced a tumbling sensation of shock. There on the wall was the patch, clearly visible even in the half-light from the hall behind me. And not only visible but larger – elongated downwards into a shape

100

like a stalactite.

I experienced something else too – a stillness so complete that I fully understood for the first time what is meant by 'dead' silence. Everything else seemed to have gone away: everything but me, and that mark on the wall, and the short space between us. My ears rang, and my legs felt like cotton wool. I tried to put out my hand to lean on the door frame but my arm was as heavy as lead. My breathing and heartbeat seemed to be happening outside me, without my direction, my body doing certain things of its own accord, refusing to do others that were asked of it.

After a time, however long it was – an eternity of seconds – everything came rushing back: the drone of the washing machine, a shout in the street, traffic sounds, the front door of the house closing. My body became once again my self, all of a piece. I leaned against the door and took long, shaky breaths. When I felt steadier I turned on the harsh overhead light. The patch was there, but dwindling almost as I looked so that it was now no more than the round area, about ten inches by ten inches, which I'd first noticed.

I made myself walk over. Nothing changed

as I did so. The living room was prosaic as ever, the patch just an unsightly mark on the naff wallpaper. Quickly, before I could change my mind, I placed my hand on it, flat, my fingers spread out. There was no moisture. The wall was dry under my palm, but very, very cold. As, I told myself, it would be if there was some submerged leak. I shivered and, as I went to remove my hand felt a slight drag, as though the fabric of the wall pressed forward, unwilling to let me go. And there was a smell – unpleasant, familiar ... drains? I didn't know. I snatched my hand away, panting, and rushed from the room, closing the door after me with the scurrying panic-stricken haste I'd employed as a child, going to bed at night spooked by the dark of the landing.

I turned on all the lights, even in the bedroom. Fortunately, nothing short of the last trump would have woken Hannah once she was asleep, and for once I was glad of the echoing ping-pong of strangers' voices across the central well. Besides being company the voices reminded me that I was part of this human termite mound, this miniature Tower of Babel. The flat was not a world unto itself, it was one cell in the whole, there must be a hundred or more factors, threads, cross-currents, links, connections in this old terrace which might cause discoloration on a wall. I remembered a comment of Anita's when we'd found mouse-droppings in our previous flat, and Hannah had wailed over the mouse-trap: 'Don't kill it, the poor little mouse!'

Anita said grimly: 'There's no such thing as one mouse, sweetie. Where there's one, there's millions, and all breeding faster than you can imagine. They haven't just picked on you, you're nothing special, they've colonized the whole damn road!'

Just then I could almost have hoped for mice, the thought of them running back and forth along the terrace was peculiarly comforting. Mice didn't care, their activities weren't circumscribed by mysteries, they'd gnaw right through my troublesome wall and out the other side if they wanted to.

I must have sat upright in bed, staring at a book, my knuckles showing white, for well over an hour before tiredness overcame my nerves and I lay down. Even then I was tense. I wished now that I hadn't closed the living room door, for what might be going on in there in the secret darkness, in the privacy that I had created? I was held in a sort of ecstasy of fear, knowing I was being irrational but unable to take the simple step which would free me.

I don't remember falling asleep, but I must have been dead to the world – weird expression – because when Hannah woke me up I was badly disorientated.

'Mum! Mu-um!' Her sharp finger prodded me in the shoulder.

'What—? Oh my God – Hannah, what time is it?'

'I don't know. Why are all the lights on?'

'I must have forgotten to – oh God, we're late, we're late, quick, get some clothes on.'

It was a horrible rush. I hated to be late, always have. Time in hand was time well spent, in my book. Lateness could sour my mood for an entire day. Hannah knew this and fell into line. We got ourselves ready on our parallel tracks without a word – scuffling, dashing, eating, slamming, and by the time we went out of the door had clawed back about fifteen minutes of the thirty we'd lost.

We got to school after the children had gone in, and I pushed poor Hannah through the doors with an exhortation to lay the blame squarely on me. Olwyn was standing outside the gate beside her car.

'Late?'

'Yes!'

'I'm going into town, can I drop you off anywhere?'

'University Street? Near Gower Street?'

'Gower Street's fine, hop in.'

It was probably no quicker travelling in Olwyn's Ka, but it relieved me of the stress of responsibility. Whatever traffic we were sitting in, it was the same that would have held up the bus, and we had no preordained stops to make. Also, I had sympathetic company.

'Thickens the arteries, doesn't it?' she observed.

'It does mine,' I admitted. 'Poor Hannah, she stresses enough without me adding to it.'

'But she's all right now isn't she?'

'Yes – yes, she is.' Much as I liked Olwyn, our friendship was not yet ready for an exchange of serious confidences. And might never be – there wasn't a single person of my acquaintance, not even Anita, whom I had told about the past. This was at least in part because once I had spoken of it I would have to assume some sort of responsibility. Not the old guilt, exactly, all current thinking would have absolved me from that, but a requirement to report, to declare, to achieve 'closure' – and I was fearful of those things. As to my odd experiences in the flat, I was busily trying to sweep those under the carpet, to persuade myself they were the product of physical and mental tiredness and my consequent overwrought imagination.

Fortunately Olwyn, if she sensed any hesitation, didn't pick up on it. She was one of those increasingly rare people prepared to take others at face value. I yielded to no-one in my affection for Anita, but she would never have let my reticence pass.

'...why not let her come back with us this afternoon?' Olwyn was saying.

'I'm sorry?'

'Hannah. Why doesn't she come and have tea with Meriel this afternoon – give you a bit of leeway at the other end of the day. Time to catch up. And anyway, you'd be doing me a favour, Meriel would love it.'

'I'm quite sure Hannah would too...' I made a quick inventory of the practicalities, but Olwyn was an experienced hand.

'You can either ring the school from work to say that it's okay, or write a little note for me to take – or both, belt and braces. And then if you give me your address, I'll run her back.'

'Oh no, that would be above and beyond

the ... I'll pick her up.'

'Okay, if that's what you'd prefer. Done.'

When we stopped in Gower Street I wrote a note for Mrs Jaynes on a spare sheet from my diary, and Olwyn wrote one for me containing her address and phone number and handed it to me, folded over.

'We're dead easy to find. Turn right out of the tube, right again, and we're facing you on the corner.'

'It's so good of you, I do appreciate it.'

'Pleasure. See you this evening – you say when.'

'Would seven be too late?'

'Absolutely not. Seven it is.'

It was only when I was walking along the road to Small World Travel that I realized I had not taken Hannah's preferences into account. What if she didn't want to go? But I told myself that she almost certainly would, and anyway I'd ring her at Meriel's to make sure.

We had a busy day and I was more than glad to have the pressure taken off the end of it. It meant I was able to clear my desk and my emails, and get a swift supermarket shop done and put away. I opened the living-room door with a sense of foreboding, and it was almost a relief to see that the patch on the wall was its usual size and shape, neither bigger nor smaller, which persuaded me that it *might* be just one of those little difficulties you had to put up with in a rented property. I put on some music and turned up the volume to keep me company as I did the chores. I promised myself that whatever belt-tightening it took – on my part, not Hannah's – I would try to get together enough for a down payment and a mortgage by the end of the following summer. And another thing – if there was one good reason for making contact with my father it was that he might, *should*, be able to help us out financially.

At six I called Olwyn. She said the girls were fine, that my daughter was 'a star' and that I should not on any account rush.

Just the same, I set off at six fifteen. It was a straight three-stop journey on the tube, but I didn't want to appear to be taking advantage first time out. When I emerged from the station the other end I followed Olwyn's instructions. It was a walk of only a few hundred yards to the corner of Norman Avenue, but a giant leap for me: Number Twenty-One, a double-fronted Edwardian detached villa with a barely controlled front garden, was also the Vicarage. I realized that didn't necessarily mean anything – most vicarages were lived in by TV producers these days. But that was in the country and wouldn't a TV producer call it the *Old Vicarage*?

As I opened the gate I did a quick mental inventory of our few conversations – had I missed something? Said anything inappropriate? Expressed contentious opinions? Endorsed pick-and-mix morality? Sworn? Too late now, anyway. But what about Hannah? She was precocious, mouthy, too much in adult company, not all of it improving ... The possibilities were petrifying.

Meriel answered the door, with Hannah close behind.

'Hallo – can she stay a bit longer, we're in the middle of *The Simpsons*?'

'Can I stay a bit longer? Please?' added Hannah.

Olwyn appeared. 'Don't worry, they haven't been in front of a screen the entire time. Come and have a drink until *The Simpsons* is finished.'

The girls returned to a playroom on the right of the front door. Olwyn led the way to a kitchen at the back. Already there were a boy of about twelve in the untucked-in white shirt and abbreviated, loosened tie of the local comprehensive, and a bald man built like an army PE instructor, wearing a T-shirt and a clerical collar on a sort of grey cotton bib. This, with the baldness and the fact that he was eating a strawberry yoghurt, combined to give the impression of a particularly sturdy baby.

'This is Adam,' said Olwyn, introducing the boy, who muttered a frowning acknowledgement and exited, carrying a plate of toast. 'And this is my husband, Phil. Phil, this is Hannah's mum, Fiona.'

He said: 'I gather our daughters have struck up a friendship.' Any fleeting resemblance to a baby was instantly dispelled by a deep, gravelly voice with an estuarine accent and a crunching handshake.

'Yes,' I replied. 'And I'm so pleased. Hannah had a bit of a rocky start at school.'

'Reuben,' explained Olwyn to her husband. 'Up to his tricks.'

Phil took off the bib and collar to reveal 'Ski Denver' emblazoned across the T-shirt.

'Will you have a glass of wine, Fiona? Any excuse. Not that we need one.'

'Thanks.'

He fetched a bottle of Italian red from a cupboard, and a corkscrew from a drawer.

'I hope you're not opening one just for

me,' I said, with unwonted delicacy. I had an agnostic's unfamiliarity with the clergy but not, I was surprised to find, the healthy disrespect that should have accompanied it.

'Don't worry.' He drew the cork with a smooth pop. 'Wine doesn't stand around unfinished in this house.'

When we all had a glass in our hands, Olwyn led the way into a big sitting room with French windows on to the garden. It was tidy – kept for best, I suspected, and the style was pleasantly chintzy and threadbare.

'You must say if you're cold,' said Olwyn.

I was rather, but didn't like to say so. 'What a fantastic house,' I said. 'I envy you all this space.'

'The C of E is a good master in that respect,' said Phil. 'But we did decide to forfeit the dining room in favour of a playroom.'

'Family room,' corrected Olwyn.

'And you're in Arbury Road,' said Phil. 'An old stamping ground of mine.'

'You know it?'

'I was there for a while as a student. Not of theology, I got the call later on in life. When I was made redundant, funnily enough. One door closes and another opens. The good Lord provides.'

I wasn't sure whether he was joking, and my uncertainty must have shown, because Olwyn said: 'It's true! The only trouble is I didn't marry a vicar.'

'So you had to retrain as well.'

'Darn right. I was a posh legal secretary believe it or not, we were the absolute acme of yuppiedom, and now look at us.'

I said, truthfully, that I was full of admiration, and then asked: 'So whereabouts were you in Arbury Road?'

'North end, near the night shelter. At the top, geographically speaking, at the bottom sociologically. But I've retained a soft spot for that area. Lots of life.'

'Yes, it has that all right.'

'Perhaps not ideal for a young family, but in those days it assisted my image of myself as an urban cowboy.'

He laughed at himself. 'How are the mighty fallen...! What a nice daughter you have there,' he continued. 'She's welcome any time.'

'Thank you. It's good to know she's okay in company.'

'So many of the kids these days don't talk. At least, not to adults. They don't *converse* if you know what I mean.'

'She spends a lot of time with adults. Too

much probably, but I'm on my own, so...'

'It's done her no harm,' said Olwyn. 'Quite the reverse. She was telling us all about your mother.'

'Really?'

'Saying how much she liked her. I mean actually liked her as opposed to just being fond of her because she was Granny. Julia, is it?'

'That's what I've always called her.'

'Why exactly?' asked Phil.

'It was what my mother wanted. Mum or Mummy just never came into it, she was always Julia, so it didn't seem in the least unusual to me.'

'Are you an only child, then?'

'Yes.'

'I only ask because parents can be a worry as they get older – my own father's on his own and keeps having accidents in the kitchen.'

I considered my mother: active, elegant, independent and due to remarry. 'I'm very fortunate. She's not a worry.'

We talked about parents, in general terms, for another ten minutes or so and then I prepared to leave. Boldly, and because I liked them, I said: 'You must come and see us in Arbury Road – visit your old haunts.'

'We'd love to, some time, when you're properly settled,' said Olwyn.

'We are. Perhaps one Sunday, for lunch—' I realized what I'd said. 'Sorry, perhaps not. One evening then. I'll give you a ring.'

Before going I arranged a return match for the following week with Meriel. On the way home I asked Hannah if she'd enjoyed herself.

'It was really, really good. Her brother's a pain, but he wasn't around much. And her Mum did sausages with Boston baked beans.'

I recognized this for the ringing encomium that it was. That night in bed I reflected on the strange turn my life had taken: there was every chance I was going to be friends with a vicar.

Eight

It's a well-known fact that time proceeds differently according to circumstances. Weekends are different from weekdays. Holidays are different from work. Childhood is different from adulthood. Time can pass slowly and disappear fast. It's a stop–start thing.

In the flat in Arbury Road, time went at a normal pace when I was with Hannah; but when I was alone, or when she was in asleep, it took on a slithering, viscous quality. When I glanced at my watch, it was always earlier than I thought. I had to consciously resist the temptation to go to bed at nine every night, not because I was tired but because I had had enough of my own company in the large, dull front room. The damp patch came and went, I'd got used to it. Or at least learned to ignore it – not to give it the satisfaction, was the phrase I used to myself, as though the stain had a presence and a personality that could be cut down to size. I tried not to let it give me the creeps. I thought about the little mice, running up and down the terrace as though they owned it, and all the pipes, and wires, and cables and joists that linked my flat with forty or so others and the people that lived in them.

But it didn't work. I was spooked. Something about this place made me feel lonely. The loneliness was reminiscent of when, as a child, I had listened to the terrible, stifled violence between my parents – a brutality muffled by my mother's overriding need for concealment, a need which gave fresh meaning to the expression 'to save face'. Then, I had been as lonely as a child could be, imprisoned by my ghastly secret. Now, I felt equally lonely – but not alone. And whatever was accompanying me here, I had yet to recognize. In the bustle and rush of the morning, and getting Hannah to school, and the business of the working day, I forgot about the flat and its strange atmosphere. But on the way home from work my slight sense of foreboding would return, no more than a shadow on the outer edges of my consciousness, and would gradually increase during the evening until, when Hannah had gone to bed, I was uncomfortable in the front room in that thick, overpowering silence which neither music nor the television could banish.

I could not avoid the simple certainty that I was not alone. I was not being neurotic. The flat was comfortable, Hannah was doing well at school, I was making new friends, I was busy at work and managing, slowly, to save. But in that high, brown room at Arbury Road, I was awaited, shadowed, and observed.

I took Hannah to the local library on Saturdays – three books and one video, DVD or tape were her ration – and one morning while she was browsing I went over to the local history section. God knows why I felt sheepish, no-one knew what I was looking up or why. There wasn't much there. I tried *Ghostly Goings On*, and a couple of photographic histories, but Arbury Road got only one mention, in connection with a fire in 1896 which had destroyed a local brewer's yard and caused terrified dray horses to charge about the streets before spreading to other buildings. A child had been killed, and a horse drowned in the canal.

The old photos fascinated me. I peered closely at the faces of shopkeepers posing proudly outside their premises, the men hatted and bewhiskered, in large, spotless aprons, their attendant women formidably strong and workmanlike. Other pictures showed popular entertainers who appeared regularly at the local music hall (where the tube station was now), a rogues' gallery of gurning, capering eccentrics in outlandish costumes. There were school photos too, and one of the inmates of an orphanage, more than a hundred children sitting at long trestles with grim-faced adults ranged around the walls. My eye ran over the rows of faces, and was caught by one of them. Prickling with apprehension, I looked more closely.

It was her – the dark-haired girl from the Foundlings Hospital. Once again she had found me, and her fierce, focused gaze held mine.

'Mum? Mum, can I have these?'

I closed the book, with all the revulsion and resistance I'd felt as a child, when asked to squash a wasp. Hannah stood next to me with an armful of stuff.

'Can I have this tape?'

She waved it at me, but I couldn't tell, and didn't care, what it was. 'Yes.'

'Can we go then?'

'Here—' I gave her her library card. 'You

take them to the desk, and I'll be there in a minute, I'm just looking at something.'

'You'll be ages!'

'No I won't – go on.'

She went to take her place in the queue, and I opened the book again, turning the pages with exquisite caution. When I came to the picture of the orphanage I scanned it quickly and found, as I feared, that this time the girl was not there. Or that I couldn't see her, it came to the same thing. There was just a sea of blank little faces paralysed by anxiety and a stoic sense of obligation ... My face felt cold and my hands trembled, I had to rest the edge of the book on the shelf to read the caption: *Children eating supper at St Agnes's Orphanage on the corner of Arbury Road and Canterwell Road, before it was destroyed by the notorious brewery fire in 1896. All the children were saved, and were accommodated in other local institutions and private homes. The orphanage, archaic even for its day, was not rebuilt.*

I re-read the caption, closed the book and pushed it back on to the shelf. Hannah had reached the front of the queue and asked, as always, to stamp her own books.

All the children were saved.

'What?' she asked.

'I didn't say anything.'

'Yes you did.'

'I must have been talking to myself.'

'Mu-um – that's the first sign of madness.'

The librarian favoured me with a roguish look. 'Out of the mouths...!'

I didn't return her smile.

That was the trouble, I suppose. The reason why I failed to make any connection between the various small but unsettling incidents that characterized those first weeks at Arbury Road. I thought it was all just *me*. That in spite of the steps forward that I'd made, I was indeed going slightly mad. Hormones, I thought, and went to the doctor with whom I'd signed on, mainly for Hannah's sake.

'I'm a bit young, surely,' I said. 'But all these mood swings, and the disturbed sleep...'

'Younger than most, certainly,' said the GP, who was several years my junior. 'But it's not uncommon for women in their early forties, or even younger, to show symptoms of menopause.' I liked the way he left out the article, said simply 'menopause', the way old Africa hands refer to 'lion'. It lent him an air of authority.

'Still,' he went on, 'I don't think it's the case with you, because apart from the poor sleep you don't seem to have any physical symptoms, and everything else you describe could be ascribed to good old twenty-first century stress.' He grinned cheerily. I didn't know what to say. I was stressed, but not in the way he meant. How could I possibly tell this scrub-headed, chambray-shirted thirty-something medic about the mark that came and went, the hand in mine, the girl who wasn't there?

'Tell you what,' he said kindly, 'let's take a blood test to be sure.'

So that's what 'we' did. Or at least, I submitted gloomily to the invasion of the needle and watched the phial fill up with my disgustingly rich, red blood. It was the sensible course of action, but I didn't want this proof of my rude health. I would not, as the doctor seemed to assume, find it reassuring. On the contrary, to be told I was robust and humming with oestrogen would only show that something else was seriously amiss.

'You did the right thing in coming to see me,' he said, holding open the door of his consulting room. 'It's always as well to eliminate certain things from the enquiries.'

★ ★ ★

When I went in for the results a week later the receptionist told me that they showed my blood to be tip-top, and that the doctor had said there was therefore no need to see him unless I specifically wanted to do so. I was being ever so gently dismissed. On the way back to the office I dropped in to Boots and bought a huge drum of capsules said to be for the 'well woman' who wanted to frolic, unfettered by cares, in the sunny uplands of early middle-age.

That was the afternoon we were having Meriel to tea. I'd arranged with Anita to leave work early so that I could pick the girls up at three thirty and not from the after-school club as I would normally have done. The minute we got back I chugged down three of the magic tablets and immediately, as one does, felt better. The sound of Hannah and Meriel larking about in the front room made everything seem normal and natural. In fact, I told myself, Hannah had never displayed the slightest anxiety about the flat, and children were supposed to be more psychically sensitive, weren't they?

They played together happily, watched a little TV and looked up Florence Nightingale and Mary Seacole on the internet while

I made spag bol. At six we all ate together at the gate-leg table. From habit, I sat with my back to the stained wall, but Hannah, making conversation as she'd been taught to do, said: 'We've got a wet patch over there, and it's getting bigger.'

'No it's not,' I said.

'It is, it's loads bigger today.'

'It comes and goes. There must be something leaky in the house next door.'

Meriel joined in. 'We had a patch on our ceiling in the kitchen and part of it fell down,' she offered enthusiastically. 'There was stuff everywhere, you could see right through.'

'Well that's not going to happen. We've had the plumber round.'

'He was useless,' said Hannah. 'You said so.'

'He checked everything. Anyway, this is a rented flat, so if the worst comes to the worst the landlord will have to sort it out.'

They were neither of them the least interested in my rationalizing, and moved on. 'Can we put a game on the computer?'

'Has everyone had enough?'

'Yes thanks.'

'Thanks for supper, spaghetti's my favourite,' said Meriel. What a nice child she was.

Unlike the whole of western civilization, or at least the whole of north London if Hannah was to be believed, we had not had a computer at home until fairly recently. Because I'd never liked the look of them and we didn't have a 'dedicated work space' in the flat, the machine sat on its horrible plastic table in an alcove at the end of the corridor, outside the bedroom door. I didn't on this occasion insist that the girls take their plates out but let them charge down there and put on the game Meriel had brought with her. I didn't, either, remark on the fact that the children weren't supposed to have computer games in school – worries about theft apparently – because it was comforting to know that even the offspring of the clergy subverted the system from time to time.

I took the dishes to the kitchen and turned on Classic FM. I'd never owned a dishwasher, but then I'd never minded washing up. It was one of those pleasantly dull domestic activities, like ironing, which could be performed on autopilot. There was the sense of doing something useful without any very great physical effort or concentration. And I liked the warmth; in the case of iron-ing the scented scorchy smell of clean clothes, and with washing up the plunging of one's hands into hot bubbles. The music was drive-time stuff, film scores and popular classics, tuneful and emotive.

The days were drawing out all the time now, the evenings growing longer and lighter, but because of the arrangement of our flat around the central well the kitchen in particular tended to be dark. Also, it was a dull, wet evening. I had no alternative but to turn on the overhead light. On the far side of the area the bedroom looked like a kind of pod, or spaceship, a central pool of drab light coming through the skylight, and a soft yellow glow from the open door into the corridor, where the girls were playing. These contrasting light sources lent the dark edges of the room an air of secrecy as though the shadows had been beaten back.

I finished the washing up, and emptied the sink. Classic FM was playing the heart-rending Rachmaninov theme from *Brief Encounter*. I took the supermarket Sauvignon from the fridge and poured myself a glass, but didn't immediately leave the kitchen. It was snug in here, tucked away from the street and with the view of my own bedroom just across the way. Fancifully I turned off the horrible striplight and stood leaning back against the work surface, sipping my wine and letting the music wash over me, bringing with it a great wave of love for my daughter. Where, I asked myself, would I be without her? She was not just my reason to get up in the morning, but my reason to keep going, to improve, to make a go of things – my *raison d'être* in fact. And good company, I increasingly realized. Most importantly, she seemed not in the least troubled by the atmosphere in the flat. Indeed she seemed not to notice an atmosphere at all.

A movement in the bedroom caught my eye – one of the girls was in there. A face appeared momentarily at the window, but before I could make out which one of them it was, it had gone again.

The kitchen light came on suddenly and I jumped, dazzled. Hannah, with Meriel in tow, came in and opened the fridge door.

'What are you doing in the dark? Is it okay if we have a toffee yoghurt?'

'I suppose ... Golly, girls, you gave me a turn. You shouldn't creep up like that.'

'We didn't.'

They took the yoghurts and I heard them go back down the passage to the computer. Whoever had been in the bedroom must have seen me standing over here in the half-light in a world of my own. But if so, they had been incredibly quick reaching the kitchen door ... I looked back across the intervening space at the bedroom. The yellow glow from the passageway filtered in from the right. I remembered now – when I had seen the girl's face at the window, that light had not been there; the room had been dark but for the faint grey funnel cast by the skylight.

Maybe, just maybe, they had switched off the light before leaving the computer, only to turn it back on when they went back.

Or maybe, as seemed increasingly likely, the face I had seen had not belonged to either of them, but to that other child. The one who was watching me across time and space, who was trying to reach me, and drawing closer all the time.

I'd always wondered what it would take to make me clean the oven before the carbon became worthy of *Time Team*. Now I knew. I re-tuned to Radio Four and the prosaic pronouncements of politicians. I put on my apron and Marigolds, kneeled down and attacked my fears with elbow grease and a substance said to be the cleaning equivalent of Semtex.

It was not Olwyn but Phil, conventionally dressed in dog collar and a grey suit, who came to collect Meriel.

'I'm sorry I'm a bit late,' he said. 'Olwyn was overtaken by events and had to pass the baton.'

'I hadn't noticed, I've had my head in the oven.'

'Not that bad, surely?'

I laughed, removing the apron and Marigolds. 'No! They've been great. Would you like a drink?'

'Well, I'm driving...' he glanced down the passage at the girls huddled round the screen, 'but since all is calm, all is bright, just a small one to fortify me for the rigours of the PCC.'

'I've got a special driver's glass.'

We took our wine into the living room, and I drew the curtains and turned on the lamps to make it cosier. The mark on the wall was almost invisible. Phil's solid masculine presence put the room in its place. Hannah appeared briefly in the doorway and then returned to Meriel. I heard her say 'It's okay, they're having a drink...'

'This is a nice flat,' he said, looking around.

'It's not bad. But my project for the year is

to buy somewhere.'

'It comes to us all, that itch to get our foot on the first rung of the dreaded property ladder. No easy task in London.'

I don't know what came over me, perhaps it was the slug of wine on my frayed nerves, but I found myself saying: 'I hope you don't mind my asking, but do you believe in ghosts?'

To his eternal credit, he didn't miss a beat. 'No.'

'But if there's an afterlife, surely?'

'Oh I believe in that, of course. Which is why I'm pretty certain souls wouldn't hang about here when they have somewhere better to go to.'

'Right.'

He peered at me encouragingly. 'Bothered about something? Or by something?'

'Actually, yes.'

'Want to talk about it, as they say on the telly?'

'It's pretty embarrassing.'

'For you, perhaps. Not for me, I promise you. I went through the embarrassment barrier years ago, it's part of the job.'

I laughed nervously. I ran the risk of spoiling an incipient friendship. But Phil was an old hand, quick to relieve my anxiety.

'Tell you what, if you do decide you'd like to chat about it, come over and see me during working hours, so to speak. Then we can be businesslike about it.'

'Yes, thank you. I might do that.'

'Give me a ring first so I can clear a decent chunk of time.'

'I will.'

Shortly after that we saw them off, I sent Hannah with oaths and imprecations to have a bath, and I returned to the cooker. By the time she emerged, the oven was equally spotless.

'Wowser, Mum,' she said. 'Can we make a cake?'

'No,' I said. 'I'm going to keep it like this. I shall never cook again.'

Worn out by my labours I watched a bit of television, and went to bed before ten. When I'd turned out the lights in the living room and was about to close the door my heart leapt halfway up my throat. For a split second I thought there was someone there, standing by the wall, looking at me.

All the time I had been sitting there, the stain had been seeping back, until it was the exact size and shape of a figure. I closed the door and ran, whimpering, to bed.

Nine

Mark Proctor and I had struck up a school-gate friendship, but I was still surprised when he asked me out. In fact it was only after I'd said yes, I would like to see the new British rom-com with him and have supper afterwards that I realized this constituted ... well, a date. I could honestly say I hadn't missed dating; I was no superannuated Bridget Jones hankering after true love (though a good shag did figure in my thoughts from time to time). The only men I wanted anything to do with were Dean and my father, and that only for Hannah's sake. From afar I looked at my mother's new relationship with a mixture of admiration and bewilderment, but certainly no envy.

Mark had booked tickets for the film at one of those new super-comfy cinemas with sofas at the back. To alleviate any anxiety I might have on that score he let me know in advance, obliquely, that we weren't on one of the sofas. 'About halfway down's right for this kind of movie,' was how he put it.

I asked Julia if she would babysit and, since she was long overdue for a visit, invited her to spend the night too. I left clean bed-clothes out for the sofa bed, and a pasta salad on the side in the kitchen. To my considerable relief she didn't, as babysitters so often do, ask if her boyfriend could come along, but arrived on the dot of six with a box of her renowned chocolate caramel slices and a DVD of the new, digitally enhanced *Bambi*. You had to hand it to her, she made a much better grandmother than she ever had a mother. Easier, I suppose.

I showed her round and she made all the right noises.

'You've got so much more space than I imagined. When you said it was just two rooms kitchen and bath, I thought golly...'

'We could have gone for a smaller place with another bedroom,' I said, fishing for reassurance.

'No, no Fee, this is heaps better. And it's nice round here, too. I've always liked this part of town.'

The extent of her denial never ceased to amaze me. This area and its associations for her must have been appalling, and yet she was able so adroitly to compartmentalize experience.

'I shan't be late,' I said. It was a promise to myself more than to her.

'Be as late as you like, we'll be happy as sandboys.'

I kissed Hannah. 'Night sweetie. Be good.'

'She always is.'

'I always am.'

Seeing Mark Proctor before he saw me in the foyer of the cinema I was forcibly reminded that he was younger than me. When we were just two parents at the school gate we took on the colouring of our surroundings. But I'd been a late starter, whereas he was an early divorcee: we were looking at forty from opposite sides. I'd gone for the default option of my best indigo jeans and needlecord jacket with a glam top and kitten heels. He was wearing slouchy chinos and a cotton sweater in washed-out pink, something, I told myself, only likely to be worn by a man super-confident in his own masculinity.

'Hallo,' he said, and then, 'Wow, lovely.'

As he said this, he touched my upper arm briefly. It was a gesture both confiding and masterful; since reading *Primary Colours* I'd become a bit of a student of body language. I noticed, too, that he smelt nice. In fact all the early signs were encouraging.

The film was very, very sentimental which might have proved awkward, but luckily it was sufficiently witty and well-directed not to descend into a slough of schmaltz and make me cry; I'd never been a pretty crier. I enjoyed the film but couldn't quite forget what I was doing, and who was next to me. I was out of practice at this sort of thing. We had never even had a conversation that wasn't in some way school- or child-related. Rather in the way that I liked to read the blurb, and so feel familiar with a book before I read it, I liked to have rather more of a handle on a man before going out with him. Beyond the fact that Mark lived in Kentish Town and worked in Human Resources he was pretty much a stranger. I had to admire his chutzpah in asking me out at all. How had he seen through the harassed, working single mother to the mature fascinator beneath?

As we shuffled our way out of the cinema, he leaned towards me: 'Don't tell me what you think till we're sitting down with a glass in our hands.'

I liked him for that – for relishing the debrief and giving it its full due. He'd also quite fortuitously picked a Turkish–Cypriot restaurant, my favourite cuisine, where all the waiters looked like bouncers and the banquettes were piled with cushions. We ordered the mezze for two and once the bottle of Othello arrived, Mark said, 'Okay, you first.'

I made a lightning decision in favour of old fashioned charm and politeness.

'I liked it a lot. An inspired choice.'

'Pretty soppy though, even by those guys' standards.'

'I don't mind soppy.'

'Nor me, in moderation. But come on, they were taking the piss this time round.'

'If they were, I didn't notice,' I said, not quite truthfully. 'It's their trademark after all, what they do best.'

'Tell me,' he leaned across confidingly. 'Would you have gone to see that on your own?'

'I don't go to the cinema on my own.'

'Honestly? I am surprised.'

'It's a social activity. Television's solitary.'

'And optional, of course.'

'Plus, I'm on my own with Hannah and babysitters are precious.'

'Tell me, have you ever walked out of a

film or a play?'

'No.'

'No matter how bad?'

'No.'

'Why not?'

'Because I always imagine that the moment I've gone they're going to get to the good bit and I'll have missed it.'

He shook his head and leaned back as the first instalment of the mezze arrived. 'I'm in the camp that says if they haven't knocked my socks off in the first three-quarters of an hour it's unlikely they're going to at all.'

'Would you have walked out tonight?' I asked, interested. 'If I hadn't been there?'

'Probably.'

'Perhaps you made the mistake of trying to guess what I'd like.'

He appeared to give this quite serious thought. 'Not that exactly. But I'd have to plead guilty to going the best loser route.'

'You could have asked me beforehand,' I suggested.

'I could,' he agreed, 'and I should have done. Next time I will.'

That 'next time' was well placed. Our little bit of fencing about the film had told us both what we wanted to know – that whatever its shortcomings this was an evening that would repay the follow-up.

A little later on, during the lamb tajine he mentioned Reuben.

'I know he can be a little bastard. I hope he didn't give your Hannah a hard time.'

'Not particularly. And anyway, she can look after herself.'

'That's what I like to hear. He needs standing up to. I only wish it wasn't necessary. It's a bloody nightmare being the parent of a troublemaker.' He rolled his eyes comically, not wanting to get too heavy. 'The guilt, oh the guilt!'

'From what I gather it's nothing serious. Nothing the others can't handle.'

'Ah!' Mark slapped his hand over his eyes. 'You gave yourself away there. "From what you gather" – how would you like it if your daughter was notorious?'

'I wouldn't,' I admitted. 'I'm sorry, I didn't mean to give that impression.'

'There may be no excuses for his behaviour, but there are reasons. He genuinely did take our break-up hard.'

'Poor kid.'

'You know what it's like, you've been through it—'

'Not really. Hannah's father buggered off before she was one year old.' I sensed we were in danger of getting into a hard luck contest, and added, 'And the awful truth is it was the best day's work he ever did, we're much better off without him.'

Mark smiled ruefully. 'If you say so.'

'He was and still is an absolute apology for a father.'

'Does he see Hannah?'

'Not for years. He went to the States and his cash went with him.'

'Bummer, I am sorry.'

'Anyway,' I said, 'I bet Reuben snaps out of it pretty soon – it's a law of diminishing returns, the less reaction he gets the less fun the provocation.'

'If you say so. Just don't invite him round. Not yet.'

I assured him that nothing could be further from my mind. When we'd had coffee I declared quite firmly that I wanted not to be home too late because my mother was babysitting – Julia might have been the dragon from hell for all he knew – and that I was going to treat myself to a cab. Out on the pavement, he at once spotted, and successfully hailed, a taxi (I like that in a man) and offered to pay, which I declined. I got in and he leaned in after me.

'Can we do this again?'

'That'd be nice.'

'I'll be in touch.'

When I got home my mother was wide awake and watching a blow-by-blow gender realignment on Channel Four.

'Can you believe it?' she said, her eyes fixed on the screen as she rose to greet me. 'Do you think it works the same?'

As she kissed me, I looked over her shoulder. The wall was completely clear. But then it wasn't Julia she was after.

I made an appointment to go and see Phil one morning when Anita had Janine's god-daughter in the office doing work experience. The god-daughter was lower sixth at St Paul's – seventeen, soignée and smart as paint. I had no qualms about being absent, in fact my only fear was that I would no longer have a job on my return.

'Come in, come in,' said Phil. 'We have the place to ourselves, will you have some coffee?'

When he'd made the coffee he carried the tray into the drawing room that we'd sat in before. I had the sense that it served the purpose of the old 'front room' or 'parlour' – reserved for best and for business.

He poured. 'Right then. The floor is yours.'

I began by trying to make a story out of it, to give the whole thing some kind of sequential, rational feel, a causality that it didn't in fact have. But I soon gave up, and by the end I was just free-associating, splurging it all out just as it occurred to me, any old how.

'Okay,' he said when I'd finished. 'Well, something's going on, for sure.'

'Yes.' I felt the most enormous relief, and gratitude that he was taking me seriously. 'It really is.'

'I know you came here for my opinion,' he said, 'but could I ask you yours?'

'How do you mean?'

'Has any explanation occurred to you, in the wee small hours? Anything at all, no matter how bizarre?'

I thought hard. 'Not really.'

'You mentioned ghosts.'

'Yes. And you said you didn't believe in them, which is perfectly understandable.'

'Hang on,' he said. 'I don't believe in them objectively – that they're out there, like pandas, and we may or may not glimpse one if we're lucky. That doesn't mean to say I don't believe certain people see them.'

'Neurotic women of a certain age,' I said snappishly before I could stop myself, and instantly regretted it. But he treated the remark as if it were perfectly routine.

'No. But there may be internal reasons for certain experiences. For instance, although you're conscious of an atmospherc in the flat, and some of the incidents you described took place there, several of them happened elsewhere. So you couldn't call the flat itself haunted.'

'I suppose not.'

'So what might the alternative be...' he mused, but I was pretty sure he already had a theory and jumped in quickly to pre-empt it.

'That I'm imagining things. Or going slightly mad.'

'Certainly not the second. And if these things – these powerful images and incidents – *are* in your imagination, then why?'

'Exactly,' I muttered.

'I have a theory, but it's only a theory. Want to hear it?'

'Please.'

'I think it's people, not places, that are haunted. And what haunts them is often some missing piece of the past.'

I considered this. 'Whose past? Their own? Or further back? Or the past of a particular place?'

'Their own past, or possibly their history. I think we like to feel part of a continuing story, and our subconscious mind or whatever is acutely aware of any gaps or dislocations, anything that's missing from the narrative.'

'It must be subconscious, because I can't think of anything. This child – this girl – she's no-one I know, or have ever heard of. Why me, for – I mean, why me? I wish she'd leave me alone.'

'Does she frighten you?'

'Yes,' I admitted. 'Yes, she does. She's so angry and needy, she desperately *wants* something from me. I can't tell you how disturbing that is. Plus, I never know where or when she's going to appear.'

'And this mark on the wall – which by the way I must say I didn't notice when I was with you the other evening – you think that's connected to the girl that you see?'

He didn't intend to make me feel stupid, but that was the effect. 'I feel as if it is. Because it comes and goes, and sometimes it's in the shape of a figure – Jesus, this sounds ridiculous – sorry.'

'Not at all, and it doesn't, not in the least. I suppose what I'm trying to point out is that when we're spooked we mustn't fall into the trap of making everything part of the spookiness. Rented flats have their idiosyncrasies, especially when they're in old buildings. You could probably eliminate the damp wall from your enquiries.'

'I had the plumber round,' I pointed out. 'And he was no help.'

'That's in the job description.'

'There was a certain amount of token grumbling. But to be fair, he seemed pretty genuine.'

'And he couldn't find anything wrong?'

'No.'

There was a short silence. I felt embarrassed, and dissatisfied, which was unreasonable since I'd never expected Phil to have a simple answer. I was grateful that he had not attempted to proselytise, on behalf of either his religion or his personal views. He had outlined his theory and left me to make up my own mind. But there was no pleasing me – childishly, I wanted to be relieved of the fear, anxiety and confusion in one fell swoop. Supremely unlikely as that always was, I now found myself wishing I'd never come.

Phil broke what was becoming an awkward silence. 'I haven't been much use to you, have I?'

It was a rhetorical question, but so uncomfortably telepathic that I felt compelled to answer. 'Not at all, no – I mean yes, you have.'

'I do believe you,' he said. I looked at him. 'Completely.'

'Thank you.'

'And I would like to help. But since I haven't got a lot of time for souls in purgatory, or hanging about in some sort of earthly waiting room, I can scarcely perform an exorcism. And even if I was disposed to, where would I do it, since it's not in your flat that the difficulty exists.'

'So tell me,' I said, 'not professionally, personally – what do you think I should do?'

'Check the story. Find out what's missing. You never know.'

'I'll try,' I said doubtfully.

'It's the best I can do,' he said.

Out in the hall, keen to get things back on a more everyday footing, and to show I wasn't completely barking, I suggested a couple of Friday dates when he and Olwyn might come to supper. As he saw me out, he said, 'Good luck. I'll stay on the case, and send one up for you.'

It was only when I was out of the house and walking down the road that I realized what he would be 'sending up' was a prayer. Had it come to this? I never thought I'd see the day when I was prayed for. Much good might it do me.

Back at the office I was informed by Anita that Annabel had been 'a complete and utter star' and had rendered me almost, but not quite, redundant. Her only shortcoming had been her glamorous appearance and toffish accent and manner, which some of our student customers had apparently found distracting.

'I did my best,' said Annabel, with a bell-like laugh. 'I can't help it.'

'I know,' said Anita, giving me a jokey look. 'We hate her, don't we Fee?'

'Yes,' I said, not as jokily as I might have done. 'We do.'

Ten

When Julia rang to tell me about my father's death, the first thing I said was:

'But I only spoke to him a couple of weeks ago...!'

The moment I'd said it I heard how ridiculous it sounded. My voice was querulous, like a peevish child's. As if the hopeless conversation I'd had with Dad could have had any bearing on the Belgian container lorry which had jack-knifed on the autoroute and swatted his cherished Riley across the carriageway like a fly.

My mother very properly let my response go without comment.

'The funeral's on Friday, near Hatfield,' she said. 'Cremation, of course. If you'd like to go, I could give you a lift.'

'You'd be going anyway, would you?'

'I think we should.'

I noted the 'we' – it was an I-will-if-you-will situation.

'It's midday,' she added encouragingly, 'so

146

there shouldn't be a problem with Hannah.'

I was more concerned about work, having only just had an unscheduled half-day off to visit Phil, but funerals were generally regarded as a special case.

'Thanks, I'll take you up on that,' I said.

It was early evening, we hadn't long been back, and Hannah was in unwind-mode in the bedroom with a Kit-Kat and Girls Aloud – very loud. I went in and waved at her to turn it off. She turned it down, a little.

'Hannah!' I bawled. 'I need to tell you something!'

'Go on then!'

'I will, but I can't hear myself think with that going on.' I pressed the button and sat down next to her on the bed. She looked at me warily from beneath her fringe.

'What?'

'That was Gran on the phone.'

'What?'

'She had some bad news, I'm afraid, darling. Granddad had an awful accident, the day before yesterday on the motorway.'

Hannah didn't move, and her expression stayed the same, but I could sense the sea-change in her, an expansion of the mental tissues to accommodate big thoughts.

'Is he dead?'

'I'm afraid – I'm afraid—' I sensed I was going to cry, and bit down hard, trying to get a grip.

'He is dead, isn't he?'

I nodded.

'Are you okay?'

That did it, and I burst into tears. Hannah knelt up and put her arms round me. We hugged as if our lives depended on it. Her grown-up composure and sympathy were both enormously touching and no good at all for what ailed me. She could never have understood the complications, fierce and sharp as a barbed-wire entanglement, in which I was enmeshed. And I could never tell her.

'Poor granddad,' she said, when I'd recovered. She was astonishing.

'At least he went out like a light.' I sniffed and dabbed. 'He won't have suffered.'

'He must have been scared.' She had the young's frank interest in gruesome details. 'He must have seen that great thing coming and tried to get out of the way.'

'It was all too quick for that,' I said, hoping it had been.

'Was Granny crying?'

'No, she wasn't. Too shocked, I expect.'

'She never cries, though, does she?'

'That's true.'

It occurred to me as I went into the kitchen to pour myself a glass of wine that I had not got round to asking my mother how she was.

Later on when Hannah had gone to bed, I called Julia back. A man's voice answered the phone, rattling off my mother's number with practised ease. Adrian.

'Hallo. May I speak to Julia?'

There was a minute hesitation. 'She can't come to the phone at the moment. Can I take a message?'

'Yes, please – this is her daughter—'

'Fiona! That's different. Adrian Downes here, by the way.'

'Hallo,' I said again.

'I know she'll want to speak to you, she's only upstairs.'

'I don't want to disturb her if she's—'

'No, no, hang on, I'll give her a shout.'

To his credit there was no covering of the mouthpiece. Obviously still holding the handset he called out: 'Jules! Jules – it's Fee on the phone for you!'

I heard my mother's faint, 'Bring it up, can you...?'

'I'm taking it up to her,' he said. 'She's in the bath.'

This, combined with the 'Jules' – no-one had ever called my mother Jules – was more information, and informality, than I was ready for.

'By the way,' said Adrian, in a suitably altered tone. 'I'm so dreadfully sorry ... About your father.'

'Thank you.' I wondered how much he knew about my mother's past. 'I've not seen him for years, but it's still a shock. Even worse for Julia, of course ... How is she?'

'Oh, philosophical as always, you know your mother – but still, I'm glad I was here when she got the news. Right, hang on, here we are...' I heard a door open, and the sound of Radio Four. 'Darling...? I'll leave you to it.' The radio was switched off, there was a faint gloop of water followed by my mother's voice.

'Hallo Fee.'

'Sorry to disturb your bath.'

'You're not, I'm lying in it.'

'Good.' I was slightly thrown by her composure and the awareness that on the other end of the line my mother was up to her neck in bubbles.

'Julia, I realized after we'd spoken that I was so caught up with my own reaction that I never asked how you were.'

'I'm fine. Honestly. Your father and I had a shared history, but that's what it has been for years now – history. He had his new life, and now I have mine. It was a shock, of course, and I'm sorry, but not sad. Not for myself. Does that sound terrible?'

'Not in the least.'

'Naomi is devastated, of course. Poor girl. It was generous of her to tell me about the funeral.'

I wanted to shriek, tear the phone from its socket, claw the walls. Instead, I said: 'Adrian sounds nice.'

'He *is* nice. You must meet him.'

'You know I spoke to Dad not long ago.'

'I didn't, till you mentioned it.'

'I thought he should see more of Hannah. Let's face it, apart from me and you, he is – he was – her only family.'

'Quite right. How did it go? Not that it makes much difference now.'

'He was busy that weekend. I said I'd get back in touch to fix a date. And then of course I didn't get round to it before – before this—' I started to wobble.

'Don't worry,' said my mother briskly. 'That's life. And death, come to that. Nothing you could have done, Fee.'

'Perhaps not, but I can't help feeling guilty.

And resentful. It's an uncomfortable combination.'

Then my mother came out with something surprising. 'You know what you'd say to me. "Let it go".'

When I didn't respond, she added: 'I hope Hannah didn't take it hard? She didn't really know him of course.'

'No, but she knows he's not there now. There's a gap in the fabric where he used to be. She's definitely thinking about it.'

'Bless her. I'll have to show her some old photographs. Even though she didn't know Miles he ought to be given his full due, if you know what I mean. So that she can picture him, and talk about her grandfather if she wants to, later on.'

I could scarcely argue with this when it was all so patently correct and appropriate.

'Of course.'

There was a long pause, as though each of us was waiting for the other to add something, then my mother said: 'Fee – I'm going to clamber out, my water's getting cold.'

'I'll say good-bye, Julia. I really only rang to check you were okay.'

'That was very filial and sweet of you. And as to Friday, the funeral, if you don't mind coming over here about nine thirty we can make a flying start.'

The moment I'd put the phone down I began to cry again, but didn't know if I was weeping for my father, my mother, Hannah, or myself. Or perhaps just for the great army of The Missing, of whom my father was now one.

On Friday morning when I presented myself at my mother's, Adrian was there. He and I stood together in the hall while she went upstairs to put on her hat. The biggest surprise was how young he was – no more than fifty, at a guess, I could just as easily have been going out with him myself. He was handsome in a traditional, clean-cut way – if I hadn't already known about the promotional videos I might have taken him for a guards officer – and had all the social graces. Here was a situation designed for maximum awkwardness, and yet he succeeded in putting me at my ease. Or at least relieved me of the responsibility of putting him at his.

'I checked the location and the route on the web,' he said, 'and downloaded it all for Julia. Not that it's very far, but on these emotionally charged expeditions the last thing one needs is any hassle about logistics.'

'Absolutely.'

'I imagine there'll be a good turn-out for your father.'

'I've really no idea. I'd lost touch with him over the years.'

He sidestepped this gracefully. 'Astonishingly, both my own parents are still going strong, in the Algarve. They're big in the expats' operatic society, next up *Carousel*.'

'Good for them.'

'Personally I couldn't stand it, but the climate's fantastic, and they have each other, so ... they're extremely fortunate.'

'How often do you see them?'

'A couple of times a year. I go there, they come here, we alternate. It's just enough, if you know what I mean. Ah!—' his face lit up with obvious pride – 'here she is.'

My mother was the epitome of appropriate chic in a fitted black suit with cream piping and a little black straw bowler.

She checked her handbag for keys, map, money, repair kit, and we left. Adrian kissed her on the lips, holding both her hands as he did so; there was no mistaking the sexual chemistry between them.

Once we were on our way I thought I'd better mention him, before he became the elephant in the living room.

'I really like him.'

'Do you?' She beamed. 'Honestly? I'm so pleased.'

'And he *really* likes you.'

'Yes...' She looked away before making a left turn. 'He does.'

'So, come on then – when will you make it official?'

'All in good time. There's no rush, after all. Let's get this sad business out of the way first.'

That irritated me. I was way too old to be put in my place by her.

'You said it yourself, Julia, it's history.'

'But today we're paying our last respects.'

The thought that she should, even retrospectively, show respect to my father left me speechless. But not entirely, I must have made some sort of stifled sound, because she glanced sharply at me.

'It's true.'

'Whatever.' I meant this to annoy, and I succeeded.

'That bloody awful expression, how I hate it! What's it supposed to mean?'

It was so unusual for my mother to swear, however mildly, that the wind went out of my sails.

'I'm sorry,' I muttered.

'Granted.'

155

'I didn't mean to be rude. Especially today.'

She fluttered a manicured hand. 'Forget it. We're on edge, the two of us. Music?'

Adrian was right, there were a lot of people at the crematorium; and I didn't know any of them. The only ones Julia recognized were Naomi, and the two or three couples who had managed the difficult balancing act of staying friends with both parties. Of this group my mother was by far the most composed. If she felt any awkwardness, she didn't show it, but sailed through the proceedings, dignified and dry-eyed.

The service, arranged by Naomi, cast an odd, sickly light on my father – the result, I couldn't help thinking, of her being so much younger, and his having shown her that side of himself that he had shown to me, his daughter. He had never, I reflected bitterly, been equipped for a mature relationship. My first reaction was that this was not what he would have chosen, but it was a reaction based on privileged information. It was certainly not what my mother would have chosen. I imagined she would have liked to see him burn in hell, with herself selling tickets for the bonfire but if this was so she didn't betray it by so much as a flicker.

We were subjected to a sentimental, faux-humanist mishmash, with an Apache blessing, a tearful encomium by Naomi herself who thanked all of us 'who loved Miles and who he loved' for being there. There was some recorded music (*Nessun Dorma* and *When I Fall in Love*) and a couple of poems. 'Do not stand at my grave and weep' and 'How do I love thee?' (Naomi again). The only hymn was 'Jerusalem' because Miles 'was a true Englishman, passionate about his country' – first I'd heard of it. Once or twice I glanced at Julia, but she appeared to be giving her undivided attention to the whole grisly business.

There was one prose reading beginning 'Death is nothing at all...' I'd only been to one other funeral in my life – my grand-mother's, when I was a child, so I wasn't familiar with the piece, but it made an impression on me. Afterwards, Julia told me that it was used a lot at funerals these days and was almost a cliché, but that didn't prevent certain lines from running through my head over and over again.

'...I have only slipped away into the next room ... Let my name be ever the household word that it was ... Life means all that it ever meant ... I am waiting for you ... somewhere very near, just round the corner ... into the next room...'

Obviously it was intended to be comforting, but I found something creepy in its insistence on the continued nearness of the departed. Plus, it was frustrating to think that even if this were so – even if Miles was just the other side of some spiritual partition, smiling his boyish smile and telling us he was the same as he'd always been – I was still not going to be able to confront him with the past, or get him to buy must-have trainers for his granddaughter. He'd been a lying, wife-beating slime-ball in life, and in death he was no different.

As the curtains drew slowly round his coffin, on which lay Naomi's wreath of cream roses, I glanced once more at my mother and was astonished to see the glimmer of a tear on her lashes. I debated whether to squeeze her hand, or put my arm round her waist, but decided against it. We didn't have that sort of relationship and she certainly wouldn't want to know that her moment of weakness had been observed.

Minutes later, as we turned to leave, there was no trace of the tear. She had somehow reabsorbed it, so her mascara would not run.

We hung about for a while outside. The only flowers had been Naomi's, which had accompanied Dad into 'the next room'. Donations had been requested to a children's charity. That had stuck in my craw, and I had not given them anything.

My mother was talking to one of the couples she knew, and I was standing by, admiring her *sangfroid*, when Naomi came over.

'Hallo, Julia...?'

'Naomi – my dear, I am so sorry.'

'It's really good of you to come. I know it would have meant a lot to Miles.'

Yeah, right, I thought – but Julia let this pass with a sympathetic smile. 'That was a lovely service. By the way, this is my daughter, Fiona.'

'Fiona, yes – we spoke on the phone...'

We shook hands. She was several years younger than me, a soft, peachy blonde in a white trouser suit.

'Are you going to come back to the George?' she enquired. 'There'll be drinks and a buffet.'

This was my mother's call, and she was smoothly decisive. 'We won't actually. But thank you.'

There was a discernible note of relief in Naomi's voice as she said good-bye, and I didn't blame her.

In the car Julia took her hat off, tossed it on to the back seat and said: 'That's better.' We drove for about half an hour, to shake off the dust of the crematorium, and stopped at a big, cheerful roadside pub for a drink and a sandwich. I ordered a coke to keep the driver company, but reckoned without Julia, who had vodka and tonic with an extra tonic on the side.

'I know, I know,' she said, 'but this will be the only one. Want to change your mind?'

'No, this is fine.'

She chugged back about a quarter of her drink. 'I'm awfully glad that's over.'

'Me too.'

I waited. I think we both knew the floor was hers. 'Very odd,' she said. 'The finality of it. That's that, he's just not there any more. No more Miles. I can stop thinking about him.'

'So you did think about him?'

'In a funny sort of way, quite a lot. What-ever I said about history, you can't just erase

160

someone you lived with for fourteen years, and knew for even longer. They become part of your make-up.'

I realized I would never have a better opportunity for a straight question.

'Were they happy years?'

'Yes of course. Never think you were the product of an unhappy marriage.' She said this firmly and quickly, but to my ears there was something artificial about the second sentence as if it had been rehearsed, at least mentally, many times.

There was a limit to how direct I could be, but I persisted. 'Was Dad good to you?'

She looked at me in surprise. 'What a funny question. He didn't have to be "good to me" as you put it. It was a marriage.'

'Does marriage mean not having to be nice to each other, then?'

'No, no,' she said with a trace of tried patience, 'but it's a partnership – equal. I wasn't some little woman who needed indulging. I could look after myself.' She must have realized how this sounded, because she added: 'We looked after each other.'

'Until he did a runner.'

She sighed, closed her eyes for a second. 'Fee, what is this?'

'I'm sorry,' I said, meaning it, but then I

was off again. 'It must be all that schmaltz back there. Who were they talking about, Julia? No-one we knew. What did bloody Miles ever do for us?'

She said quietly: 'He did his best.'

Yeah, right. 'Or for Hannah?'

'Well, I admit ... But he was long gone by then. He never met her.'

'He never tried!'

Julia rotated her glass slowly between her fingers on the table. 'That's true. But you were doing something about that, and from what you say he was pleased you were in touch. He was always a *reactive* sort of man. And he didn't plan to get wiped out by a lorry.'

Our sandwiches arrived and we sat staring at them for a moment as if they were some token from another planet. They were also the cue for a change of conversational gear – what with one thing and another we were starving, and it was impossible to discuss heavy stuff while eating.

But when we were back in the car Julia returned briefly to the subject.

'Fee,' she said, 'please don't ask me to speak ill of him. Not today.'

As we pulled out into the road she added, almost as an afterthought: 'Not ever.'

Eleven

The few days between my father's death and his funeral had been notable for the absence of any troubling phenomena. I imagined, fancifully, that they'd been temporarily seen off by the shock of real events.

The weekend after the funeral the weather, which until now had been cool and uncertain, changed. A brassy sun elbowed aside the clouds and took the stage. London shimmered and growled under a heatwave. To begin with the change was welcome. About time, everyone agreed; it was the end of June, midsummer for heaven's sake, and we were entitled to some sunshine. The days were at their longest and I yearned for an outdoor space of our own where we could sit and breathe in the heady neighbourhood mixture of traffic fumes, cooking and garden smells. Often we did the next best thing and took a picnic supper over to the park, throwing bits of quiche to the ducks and playing

Frisbee.

As the heatwave crawled on, so the flat once more became oppressive. It wasn't just that it was hot – it was stifling. Because of the arrangement of rooms around the building's central well, I couldn't get any fresh air circulating. I flung open windows, but they were like gasping mouths, taking in even more of the stale, polluted city heat. I tried the alternative – keeping the windows closed and the curtains drawn during the day, but getting back to darkened rooms in the middle of summer was depressing, and I always gave in to the urge to throw everything wide again and reverse any beneficial effects.

Besides, it wasn't only the heat that was making the flat uncomfortable. My fellow traveller had retreated for a while, but now she was back. The long, light evenings made no difference. Once Hannah was in bed I was once again subject to that sticky veil of silence which cut me off, no matter how many people went about their business in the street only a few feet away. The stain on the wall returned and was more than ever like a figure, not always in the same position, but distinct.

I'd been out with Mark again, three times. We'd seen another film, been to the Street of

Curries in Stoke Newington, and caroused at a pub with Irish music – Mark had a microscopic drop of Irish blood and I'd always been susceptible to Celticness in all its forms, so we sang along like good 'uns. On all of these occasions my mother baby-sat. On the fourth date, well into the heat-wave, it was supposed to be Anita but when I opened the door there was Janine, formidably businesslike in her black suit, briefcase in hand.

'Sorry,' she said, 'our girl's nursing a raging abscess on her tooth, so you've got me.'

'Janine, you should have rung, you don't have to do this, I can't possibly—'

She stepped firmly over the threshold. 'Just show me where you keep the coffee, leave your mobile number and clear off.'

Hannah appeared. 'Hi! Are you looking after me?'

'No,' said Janine, 'you're going to look after me.'

'You're to be very, very good,' I said, 'and do exactly as Janine says.'

'Where's Anita?'

'She's really fed up not to be here,' said Janine, 'believe it or not this is one occasion when you'll be better off with me.'

'Cool,' said Hannah.

Janine glanced at her watch, then at me. 'Off you go. Hannah can show me round.'

I hadn't yet slept with Mark. One of the advantages of Janine replacing Anita was that she would not quiz me about this on my return. Anita was frankly astonished at my tardiness. The truth was I was nervous. I was going to need an awful lot of time and re-assurance – wooing, in fact – before I was ready to expose my forty-year-old body to the male gaze. Also, I had become used to a self-contained, self-sufficient life. Sleeping with Mark would not just admit him, it would admit to something in me – a basic human need I was in the habit, these days, of denying.

Whatever my thoughts and feelings, there was no doubt about his. He had declared himself on date three.

'This isn't just a friendship,' he said, 'not for me, anyway.'

I was flattered, but slightly shocked, as though he'd broken the terms of some unspoken agreement.

'So what is it?' I asked.

'Nothing new and original.' He smiled, and shrugged. 'I fancy you ferociously. Everything about you. You're so gorgeous and smart and go-hang.'

It was my turn to laugh. 'Go-hang? Is that good?'

'It drives me wild, I can tell you.'

'And there was me thinking I was warm, charming and approachable.'

'Two out of three ain't bad.'

That night he drove me home. I explained that I wasn't going to ask him in because my mother was there, so he kissed me in the car. It was exciting, slightly awkward and teenager-y. The old song had it right: 'It's in his kiss'. The moment your mouth comes into contact with someone else's is the moment you know what the possibilities are, or if there are any at all. This kiss told me that whatever my psychological reservations about the next step, my body was ready to party with Mark's, any time.

Tonight, as it was so hot, he'd invited me to supper at his flat – he had a shady patio, he said, that was like an oasis, and he'd really like to cook for me. This, I told myself, could be decision time. When I left Janine and Hannah at Arbury Road there was a condom in my handbag – a span-new one, not the one I'd carried around in my make-up bag for the past ten years.

167

Mark greeted me wearing well-worn jeans, deck shoes, and a white collarless shirt, untucked – I liked that. He put his hands on my shoulders and kissed me lightly on the lips.

'I can't tell you how I've been looking forward to this.'

'And me.' I handed him the bottle of wine I'd brought. I'd agonized over it more than he would ever know. 'Hope this is all right. If not, you can always give it—'

'Brilliant. We're having pasta, so a nice juicy Italian red's perfect.'

His flat was narrow and dark, but I scarcely noticed because we went straight through to the kitchen at the back (I had a brief glimpse of inviting things in preparation – basil, tomatoes, olive oil, cheese) and out the other side. He was right – the patio was an oasis. In any normal English summer you'd have considered it too shady. But this evening the screening shrubs and potted palms, the tall fan-shaped ferns, the trellis and fence shrouded in climbing plants, provided a cool, fragrant sanctuary from the sun.

There was a small wooden table set up on the terracotta tiles, on which lay a hand-painted tray with two champagne flutes and a bowl of olives. Mark sat me down on a wicker chair with a bleached and tattered cushion, and went back into the flat, returning a moment later with a chilled bottle of *prosecco*.

'Aperitif,' he said, 'we'll drink yours with dinner.'

'This is absolutely lovely,' I said.

'It's what sold me the flat. I came to see it on a nice day, and this was the very occasion I pictured. The flat's nothing to write home about, just functional, but out here's the business.' He raised his glass in my direction. 'And having you here completes it.'

'Is Reuben around?'

'No!' He barked with laughter. 'Jesus! I wouldn't wish that on my worst enemy, let alone the woman I want to impress. No, he's with his mother. I'm alternate weekends and as and when in between.'

'You're a good dad,' I said.

'I am a *dad*,' he conceded, 'but a pretty average one. I hope he isn't still giving Hannah a hard time, he can be such a little thug.'

'Everything's fine now,' I said.

'I'm pleased to hear it. Fee—'

'Yes?'

'This is the first I've seen you since you told me about your father. I'm so sorry.'

'Thanks,' I said, 'but I'm absolutely okay about it. I hadn't seen him in years, so we didn't have a relationship to speak of.'

'But you must have, once.'

'A long time ago. Look, Mark...' Suddenly I realized that I couldn't deal with his sympathy, face to face like this. He was being kind, but it didn't feel right, everything was too complicated and I couldn't possibly explain. 'Don't let's talk about that.'

'I'm sorry.'

'No, it was kind of you, but – let's leave it.'

'You got it, as they say.'

In its way this pact, easily and mutually agreed upon, made us more relaxed with one another. My reticence and his acceptance of it was a sign of our increasing closeness, and of the fact that we had time. There would be another, better moment for us to have that particular conversation.

We ate outside at the little table, with the dishes of pasta and salad balanced on an upturned cardboard carton. The food Mark made was simple and peasanty with clear, bright tastes and no frills. When we'd finished, and I complimented him on it, he said, 'One good thing about being on my own again is the cooking. I've always enjoyed it, and suspected I'd be a dab hand given the chance, but Maggie was an exceptional cook so I didn't often get near the kitchen. Now I'm on my own I can cook to my heart's content. But it's a lot more fun cooking for other people. Especially someone like you. So you're indulging me.'

I smiled. 'Any time.'

'You mean that?'

'Yes,' I said steadily. 'Yes, I do.'

'In that case...' He reached out and claimed my hand – holding it in both of his. 'How about – right now?'

I suppose I had imagined a more gradual edging towards the bedroom, the two of us transcended and transported by passion, incapable of rational thought, shedding clothes as we went like the couple in that romantic comedy we'd been to see on our first date. Instead of which I was being put fairly and squarely on the spot. There was to be no fudging of the issue. This would happen if I wanted it to, and not if I didn't. What's more, there was no pressure. I knew that if I refused, the evening would not come to an end, but continue just as pleasantly, without resentment. This was grown-up time.

Mark still had hold of my hand. Now he lifted it to his lips, and looked at me over his kiss, his eyebrows lifted slightly.

As firmly as he had taken my hand, I withdrew it, and got to my feet. I could see in his face the swift beat of disappointment, instantly stifled. He rose as well, and said: 'Don't go Fee, please. It's so great just having you here.'

'I'm not going anywhere,' I said, 'unless you come with me.'

A peeping Tom, observing us in the bedroom, might have taken us, to begin with anyway, for a married couple. We undressed separately, and quietly, put our clothes on the chair, and Mark rolled back the duvet. Then we lay down together on the cool, smooth sheet and began the leisurely, luxurious process of mutual exploration. There was that sense, again, of time in hand. Faith in the future.

As my hand moved over this stranger's skin, two lines from a poem I'd come across in school, and didn't know I'd remembered, flitted into my mind: 'Oh my America, my new-found land...'

After we made love we lay and talked, desultorily, for a while, and then made love once more, and slightly differently, sealing and confirming what had happened between us.

It was ten thirty and I had to go. Mark went to shower and call me a cab which he insisted he would pay for. I lay there, heavy and satisfied, yet feeling as though I were floating in the thick, warm dusk. The bedroom had a rattan blind which gave the twilight a sepia glow. For a moment, I dozed.

Something woke me up. My eyes snapped open. It wasn't Mark, I could still hear the gush of the shower. I was lying on my side, facing into the centre of the bed, but now I rolled over.

There, right in front of me and at eye level, was a face. The face of the girl. She was so close that I could see the way the individual hairs sprang from the pale skin at her hair-line, and the tiny lines on her lower lip. Her eyes were enormous and dark, staring at me and through me with a fierce, imperious pleading. A smell, the one I'd noticed once before, emanated from her, sweetish yet sickly, filling my nostrils and bringing the saliva into my mouth; unidentifiable but horribly familiar. I had never before understood the phrase 'paralysed with fear'. Now I was petrified, unable to move, or make a sound – scarcely even able to breathe. It was not just her presence and extreme proximity that were so terrifying. To be at this level she must be kneeling. She must have advanced across the room – from wherever she had come from – and knelt down by the bed, the better to scrutinize me, waiting for me to turn and see her. Or perhaps preparing to reach out and touch...

I tried to move my lips. To say: 'What do you want?' But it was as if my face and all its muscles had become subsumed in hers. Like the time I had put my hand against the wall, and felt it cling and suck at my palm, unwilling to let me go. She moved closer; her face, with those great hypnotic, demanding eyes, swam towards me, the smell filled my nostrils.

'Fee?'

There was a great bang! in my head and I seemed to be falling, tumbling, as if I'd stepped over a cliff. The voice I'd been unable to find burst out of me in an explosive animal scream.

'Fee – darling! Easy!'

It was Mark, scooping me into his arms, engulfing me in his warm reality, and I clung to him, gasping for breath, shaken and shaking.

He was laughing. Laughing! 'You jumped

out of your skin. I'm so sorry – I can't say I didn't mean to creep up on you, because I did, and with the worst possible intentions. But I really didn't mean to scare the bejasus out of you. How unflattering is that?'

I didn't say anything – I couldn't. For a full minute I huddled in his embrace. He accepted my shuddering silence and was quiet himself, stroking my hair. When I'd calmed down, I extricated myself, not meeting his eye, scrambled back into my clothes and went into the kitchen. Mark poured us both another glass of wine.

'Cab'll be here in fifteen minutes. Sure you don't want a shower, to wash away the horrors – or what about a nice hot bath? I bought Penhaligon's Bluebell in your honour, and the cab can sit for a bit.'

I didn't feel strong enough to comment on his slightly over-confident purchase of expensive bath oil.

'No, that's fine. Sorry I got in such a state. I was dreaming, and then when you woke me up, I felt I was falling.'

'That's a bugger. I often get it as I'm about to drop off – in fact, dropping off describes it pretty accurately, like stepping into thin air.'

'That's right.'

The words sounded faint and flat. I seemed to have gone slightly deaf, as when I'd had an ear infection as a child, and my voice had become distant from me. Incredibly, on this sultry night, I was shivering with cold. I sat down abruptly on one of the kitchen chairs. I felt queasy and pushed my wine glass away.

'Are you sure you're all right?' Mark put down his own glass and pulled a chair alongside mine. 'You look quite peaky.'

I was about to tell him how perfectly okay I was when my mouth filled with bile and my stomach contracted. I only just made the lavatory in time, my noisy vomiting made worse by the knowledge that he could hear every last, humiliating retch, heave and spit. I hadn't turned the light on, and when I thought I'd thrown up all I could – so much for the delicious supper – I heeled the door shut behind me.

It was as I kneeled there in the dark, embracing the bowl, too weak and shattered even to cry, that I felt a small, cool hand brush my hair back from my face and tuck it, solicitously, behind my ear...

'No!' I sobbed. 'Please don't. Please go away! Stay away from me...!'

'Fee?' Mark tapped on the door. 'Are you

okay?'

'Yes – I will be—' I scrabbled at the toilet roll, pulled off a length and wiped my face. 'I'll be out in a minute.'

'No rush,' he said. Did I detect a note of wariness? Poor bloke. 'Take your time.'

I sloshed cold water over my face, rinsed out my mouth and looked at myself in the mirror. Unfortunately it was no longer re-motely funny to compare my pallid, horror-struck reflection with a ghost. My hair was smoothed back off my face and tucked behind my ears.

When I came out, Mark was making not-in-the-least-bothered-by-all-this sounds in the kitchen. When I went in he said cheer-fully, 'Cab's here,' before turning round. On seeing me he said nothing but came and put his arms round me.

'Yes,' he said. 'Home. And bed.'

Janine had pulled the standard lamp out as far as it would go, moved the armchair to meet it, and was reading legal papers: a file with pink legal tape lay on the floor next to her. Classic FM was well into its late night world-music zone. She did that nice thing of barely looking up as I came in, to show how unfussed she was about the timing of my return.

'Hi ... Have fun?'

'Janine – I'm so sorry I'm late.'

'Are you?'

'You know I am.'

'I haven't been clock-watching. The time's passed very pleasantly.' She shuffled the papers together and replaced them in the file. Then she took off her reading glasses to refocus on me. She frowned. 'Fee, I hope I'm not stepping out of line, but are you all right?'

'No, that's just the thing, I haven't been. It was quite sudden, after dinner – I had to come home in a taxi.'

'Something you ate?'

'I don't know. It might have been.'

'Anyway,' she got up and put her glasses in their case, and the file in her briefcase, 'who cares? You need to get to bed and I shall make myself scarce.'

I followed her into the hall. 'Janine, this was so kind of you.'

'My pleasure. Any time. Your daughter is excellent company.'

'I'm glad you thought so.'

'I did. She was.' Janine opened the door, and gave me a perspicacious look, eyebrows raised. 'Anyway, apart from all that, how was it?'

'A lovely evening, right up till almost the last minute.'

'So your indisposition didn't spoil – anything?'

I smiled, albeit a trifle wanly. 'No.'

'Delighted to hear it. We'll ring tomorrow to see how you are. Sleep well.'

'Good night Janine.'

When she'd gone I hurried round, turning off the lights and closing the living room door, looking neither to right nor left. I cleaned my teeth with harsh thoroughness, and got into bed, leaving the bedside lamp on, and also the radio, clattering with comedy. Phil had been right; it was no one place that was haunted, it was me.

When the phone rang I didn't answer it. I lay staring up at the skylight, my breathing shallow until at some point, during the syrupy strings of 'Sailing By', I lost con- sciousness.

Twelve

'July the twentieth,' said my mother.

'Gosh – that's only about four weeks.'

'There seemed no reason to wait. We'd have made it sooner, but we wanted to book the Chantry. Because of the short notice, they could only offer a weekday, I hope that won't make a difference.'

'Julia! This is your wedding we're talking about. My mother's big day. We shall be there!'

'Of course you will.'

I realized that so far I had omitted to say the most important thing.

'And it's fantastic news, I'm so pleased for you. For both of you.'

'Thank you. I just – I just do *hope* that people won't think the wrong thing. So soon after the death of your father...'

She sounded uncharacteristically hesitant, and I tried unsuccessfully not to sound irritated. 'Julia! For one thing, Dad left you donkey's years ago, and had already made a new life for himself. For another, who cares what people think?'

'You misunderstand me,' she said, a more familiar steely note in her voice. 'I wouldn't want anyone to be under the impression I'd been carrying some sort of torch all these years. That I was marrying for that reason. That wouldn't do at all.'

She was, and always had been, so hard to read. I couldn't tell whether this speech represented the unvarnished truth, or a defence mechanism, or if she was shutting the door in my face; which would be scarcely fair since it was she who had expressed doubt and I'd been only trying to reassure her.

I said coolly, 'I'm sure they won't think that.'

She moved on at once to other things, telling me that they would only be inviting twenty or so people to the wedding and that it would all be very 'low-key and grown-up' as she put it, with the ceremony in the Chantry being followed by lunch at the nearby Host's Arms, holder of two Michelin stars.

'Something extremely plain,' she said, in answer to my question about her dress. 'I don't want to make the mistake of being too bridal at my age.'

'You could never do that,' I said. 'You're the most elegant woman I know.'

'I'll accept the compliment gracefully, but you can't be too careful. Anyway, you must let me buy you and Hannah something new for the occasion. Go and have a shop and send me the bill.'

She mentioned a sum way outside our normal range, and I thanked her profusely. Hannah, I knew, would be unequivocally delighted. For myself, I couldn't banish the ignoble thought that my mother wanted to ensure I was smart on her big day. I had never aspired to, nor achieved, her level of chic.

Telepathically, she added: 'Whatever will make you happy. There's no dress code, we want everyone to be themselves.'

'Good on her,' said Anita, who approved of my mother. 'And about time too. Is he nice?'

'I think so. I hardly know him.'

'Attractive?'

'She certainly thinks so—'

'What about you?'

'He's good-looking. Lots of charm—'

'Whoah ... suspect thing, charm.'

'It seems natural. No, he's okay. A nice man who dotes on her, just what she needs.'

Anita and I were reorganizing the window at Small World Travel, putting up the latest cheapos and good offers. Gap year season was here again and the less organised students were trickling in looking to put the greatest distance, at the least cost, between themselves and the consequences of their upcoming exam results. I came from the generation before the phrase 'gap year' entered the language. Then, it had been called 'taking a year off', and was for the irresponsible, the adventurous, or the unashamedly well to do. Now, there were whole companies devoted to helping parents and offspring with destinations, employment, bureaucracy, health, safety and communications during this important time, and to relieving them of their money in the process. Organized families used these companies. We got the last minute scrabblers, the escape artists and the latter-day hippies. It would have been very easy to take advantage of them, to rip them off, but we didn't. Anita was a shrewd businesswoman but also a principled one, and everyone got a good service. Once every eighteen months she and Janine took off and checked out various destinations – with one or two comfortable hotels thrown in – and we published the fruits of their research in our very own desk-top rough guide.

She'd asked me more than once if I'd like to go on one of these field trips, but I'd always said no, because of Hannah. Recently, she was becoming so independent that I'd found myself entertaining the idea as a real possibility, not perhaps for the four or five weeks that Anita and Janine undertook, but for a more limited period, during which Hannah could go to my mother. Today I considered gloomily that I'd probably left it too late. Julia wasn't going to want residential child-minding so soon after her marriage, and I had no idea what Adrian's attitude was. Beneath his affability he could be a child-hating domestic tyrant for all I knew.

I wasn't going to be allowed to get my irksome thoughts about child-minding out of my head. When we'd finished the window and I went out to put the kettle on for coffee, Kenny, undisputed *uber*-nerd of our little empire, was on the computer in the back office.

'By the way, Fee,' he said, 'any idea when you'd like to take the rest of your holiday?'

'None at all, I'm afraid.'

'For instance,' said Kenny, 'when does school break up?'

'Fourth week in July, I imagine.'

'August, then?'

'I suppose so – look, Kenny, can we sort this out another time?'

'Sure.' He looked slightly huffy. 'I just don't want you to lose out.'

This was bullshit – all he wanted was to fill in his wretched chart. But he'd picked the wrong woman, I wasn't going to be bounced into a premature decision for the sake of his job satisfaction.

'Don't worry Kenny,' I said. 'I won't.'

Still more annoyingly, Kenny had reminded me that whatever I was doing in August I was probably going to have a child-minding problem. I didn't know any of my neighbours well enough, and if I had doubts about Julia and Adrian having Hannah for two weeks, how much less likely were they to want to step into the breach for six, in the first tender flush of their marriage. I hadn't paid for help since the Gloria days, but it looked as if I'd have to now.

It wasn't only Kenny's officiousness that made me irritable. I was sleeping poorly, and constantly anxious. I avoided mirrors as much as possible, but when I did catch sight of my reflection I would have done nicely for the 'before' picture in a painkiller advertisement. Tense, nervous headache? I had one almost permanently. There had been no repeat of the incident at Mark's, thank God, nor anything like it, but the atmosphere in the flat continued to be oppressive. I had no privacy. Not knowing when something might happen, I could never relax. I only felt safe in Hannah's company; her presence kept the horrors at bay, so I tended to let her stay up till nine, and go to bed at the same time. This helped me a little, but wasn't good for her. Mrs Jaynes waylaid me when I picked up Hannah from after-school club and enquired discreetly whether Hannah was getting enough sleep.

'Only she seems rather tired. Her eyelids were literally drooping in class this morning, and that's not like her. You know your daughter – a live wire.'

I was at once awash with guilt. 'I'm so sorry, that's my fault. I think I have probably been getting in the habit of letting her stay up too late.'

'It's difficult, I know.' Mrs Jaynes smiled a knowing, sympathetic smile. 'They know how to keep the pressure up. My oldest boy was hyperactive and getting him into bed at all was a complete nightmare. But during the school week try and stick to your guns. Apart from anything else, you need a bit of evening to yourself.'

Oh the irony! I agreed with her of course, and let Hannah take the blame for my own cringing weakness. Worried and weepy, living on my nerves, I began to wonder if I could be clinically depressed. I longed to be away from the flat, but had no energy to go and look for anywhere else

Mark rang me several times to see how I was, and a week later I asked him round to have supper with Phil and Olwyn, since I knew they all liked each other and the Owens weren't gossips.

'As co-host,' he said, 'is there anything I can bring with me?'

'Some wine,' I suggested.

'Leave it with me. There's an Italian *gelateria* near me, would you like some wicked ice cream for afters?'

'That would be great.'

I arranged for Hannah to go to my mother's – it was a good way of testing the premarital water. Happily, she was particularly welcoming.

'Lovely – we'll both be here, so she can get

to know Adrian a bit.'

'Are you sure you don't mind? She won't be intruding on your evening?'

'Of course not! We'd be delighted. And Fee—'

'Yes?'

'If you need help during the school holidays – well, I won't say nothing's changed, because of course it has, but do call on me. Perhaps not every day, you know, but—'

'Julia!' I practically wept with gratitude. 'You are a complete star!'

'Hardly,' said my mother dryly, 'but a dependable grandparent, I hope.'

Julia had offered to pick Hannah up from school on the night of the supper party, and I'd asked Mark to arrive early. I'd made a salad niçoise for starters and there was a leg of lamb in the oven, cooking in the Greek manner: crisp and well done with aubergines, courgettes and new potatoes. The empty flat always drove me into a ferment of activity, so I was fully prepared when Mark duly showed up at six thirty, with four bottles of wine and a litre of Italian ice cream, half pistachio and half double chocolate. Even the table was laid, right down to my seldom-used Japanese dish with floating nightlights and flower heads.

'Wow, you've been busy,' he said. 'You've made it all look so pretty and inviting. I'd mention a woman's touch if I didn't think you'd swipe me with your handbag.'

'This flat's a bit stark, it needs something.'

'And you,' he said, taking me in his arms, 'have provided it. What time are they coming?'

'Seven thirty for eight.'

'In that case ... How about the perfect start to the evening?'

It was the perfect start, and for me at least, it helped if not to banish, at least to distance, what had happened before. In the early evening the bedroom, with its big skylight, was hot and brilliantly light. Afterwards, as I tidied up my make-up and hair, Mark lay with his arms behind his head and ankles crossed, gazing up at the skylight.

'This room isn't stark,' he said. 'It's grand and unusual.'

I agreed. 'Your garden was what sold your place to you. This room did it for me. I only wish I could find a way of getting the glass cleaned.'

'There's no access from here?'

'From anywhere. You'd have to be winched down from a helicopter.'

'In that case, much as I would like to be your handyman, I shan't offer...'

I sprayed myself with my only expensive scent, the carefully husbanded fruits of my last airport visit.

'Gorgeous smell. What do you use?' Mark asked.

'Romance, by Ralph Lauren.'

'I'll get you a vat of the stuff.'

I went over to the bed and sat down next to him, laying a hand on his chest. He grabbed my hand and placed it firmly over his cock, which was once more ready for anything.

'There isn't time,' I protested.

'Just passing a pretty compliment. Or at the very least a token of my ungovernable lust.'

I fell into his embrace. We made time.

As he clambered into his clothes, he glanced upwards again, and said: 'You know the one thing that would bother me about that?'

I was on my way out of the door, but leaned back in for a moment. 'What?'

'I'd keep expecting to see someone watching me.'

'Keep your exhibitionist fantasies to yourself!'

I laughed, but I wished – how I wished – that he hadn't said it.

The evening was a great success. Because I'd kept the food itself simple, there was nothing to worry about, or to go wrong: it was delicious. The wine flowed, the conversation bubbled merrily, the atmosphere grew increasingly convivial, and I experienced the kind of sense of well-being which had been notably absent from my life for the past couple of months. *That* was the trouble, I reflected boozily – I hadn't had enough fun in my life. It wasn't good for a person to be too much in their own company, my imagination had gone into overdrive. I had a good job, new friends, and most importantly a man whom I not only lusted after, but might be falling in love with. Happiness was in the air.

So when Phil raised the question of my worries, I was in no mood to discuss them. He'd followed me out to the kitchen with the cheese plates, and was leaning on the counter while I put on the kettle and arranged coffee cups on a tray.

'Wonderful evening,' he said. 'Thanks so much for asking us.'

'A pleasure,' I replied truthfully, 'it's done

me the power of good.'

I knew what was coming next. 'Everything okay?'

'Yes.'

'I'm afraid I wasn't much help – before, when you came round. I wasn't what you needed.'

'You were. You listened, and took me seriously.'

'Any more episodes?'

I didn't want to lie to him, but even less did I want to talk about it and thereby raise, literally, a spectre at my feast.

'Not really.'

'Good.' He tapped the work-top as though placing a full stop on the conversation. 'Glad to hear it. Anyway, you know where I am.'

'Thanks, Phil. Sugar – it's in that bowl.'

He passed it. 'It's good to meet Mark. Properly, rather than just at the school gate.'

'Yes. Here—' I handed him the tray – 'do you mind taking this?'

Our eyes met and his face was such a study in neutrality that I had to laugh. 'And yes, we're—' I paused. What were we doing?

'Dating?' Phil suggested.

'Dating. Exactly.'

'Splendid. Do you want to put those chocolates on while we're at it?'

So, in the space of a few slightly drunken minutes in the kitchen I had given Phil to believe that there was nothing wrong, that I was *over all that* and on to the next thing in the shape of a revived love life.

All I can say now, is that was how I felt at the time.

The next morning I had a hangover like a car crash, with all the attendant symptoms – pounding head, churning stomach, and the most appalling boozer's gloom. Mark left at six, when I was barely sentient. This was a good thing as I almost certainly looked marginally better horizontal under the duvet than vertical, red-eyed and dog-breathed, with gravity exerting its pull on my dehydrated tissues.

It was Friday, and I had to get to work. At about eight I dragged myself out of bed and shuffled, like the undead, in the direction of the kitchen. At least, thanks to well-behaved guests, most of the clearing up was done. I had no intention of doing any more till I got back this evening. Hannah, I told myself vaguely, could help.

I made myself a large mug of strong brown tea with two sugars and went to sit down in the living room. The curtains were still drawn and the air reeked of stale jollity – there are few more desolate odours than that of last night's party. I put down my mug and went over to the window, shielding my eyes as I pulled back the curtains, in expectation of what had become the usual unforgiving glare of sunlight. But incredibly, it was overcast. I pulled the top of the window down as far as I could. There was no change in the temperature, if anything it felt even hotter, and heavier – as though the flat, opaque clouds that masked the sky were sucking the oxygen from the atmosphere. Unusually for this time on a weekday morning there was no-one in the street. I might have been the only person there.

But when I turned back, I was not alone. The girl was standing in her place by the wall, watching me, as she must have been since I walked in. Somehow, ill and befuddled as I felt, I managed to take a couple of steps towards her. Still she didn't move. I found myself thinking – if I reach her, how will she feel? What will it be like? And then I remembered that we knew each other well. I had felt her hand in mine, and her fingers stroking back my hair. And now that smell was in the room again, drowning out all the others, in spite of the open window: thick, sickly sweet and sensuous, so maddeningly hard to identify.

I took one more step and then, as before, it was a noise – this time the whine of a motorbike in the street outside – that broke the spell and I seemed to fall, to burst through the silence into another room, which no longer contained the girl.

Panting and faint, my head spinning, I collapsed on the sofa. The wall bore, unmistakably, her fading outline.

Thirteen

All that day the sky was overcast, and the heat intensified. At work I felt terrible and looked at least as bad as I felt. I was exhausted, and my headache was way beyond one any hangover could justify. At one o'clock Anita tried to send me home.

'Go on, for God's sake – we're not busy, and frankly you're making me nervous.'

'No, no – I'll put my head down for half an hour and I'll be fine.'

'Go and do it somewhere else. It's an order.'

Tears of humiliation pricked my eyes. 'I am sorry.'

She gave me a wry look. 'Must have been a good night.'

'It was, but it's not that, it can't possibly be ... I think I must have a bug of some sort.'

'In that case, all the more reason to fuck off home, and take the wretched thing with you. We don't want it do we, Kenny?'

'No we don't!' said Kenny. 'I've got a blue-grass festival this weekend, thank you very much.'

That was a low blow, siding with Kenny against me, and Anita knew it. I slunk off. But the moment I was outside I knew I couldn't face going back to the flat. Quite apart from the mess that would have to be dealt with, in those rooms there was nothing to stand between the girl and me. For she would show herself, I was sure of that, and the thought terrified me. I was helpless in the face of her demanding presence, and dreadfully afraid of what her next step might be. She had singled me out, she wanted something, but I didn't know what, nor even if it was in my power to give it her.

I walked, light-headed and almost reeling

196

with tiredness, in the general direction of home. When I hit the local high road, the scruffy bustle which I generally found fun and invigorating broke over me in a wave of Hogarthian nastiness – every face was ugly, every noise harsh, every smell disgusting – and I turned off and headed for the little public gardens that I'd seen before. It was a haven of tranquil respectability, with seats set at intervals beside the circular path, flowerbeds bright with well-disciplined municipal blooms, and, most importantly, half a dozen great, sheltering trees.

There were very few people in the garden: an old lady bent over like a human question mark, with a small, waddling dog on a lead; a couple of schoolgirls sitting cross-legged on the grass, talking on mobile phones; and a man in council overalls with a barrow, trawling for litter.

I headed for the nearest seat and plumped down. This was what I needed – coolness, and rest, and the company of strangers.

I glanced dully around the square. Two sides were terraced houses, similar but superior to Arbury Road – mostly red brick picked out in white, with the odd window box and mansard development. The side nearest the high road was made up of a row of small businesses: a dry cleaner, a ticket agency, newsagent, greengrocer, minicab office and a couple of fast-food outlets. The fourth side – furthest from where I sat – comprised a large building in a rather pompous, Victorian, quasi-Palladian style, with the words *Ars longa, vita brevis* carved over the portico of the main door. Some kind of college, I guessed. Between that and a brutalist office block was a church, narrow and old, its spire dwarfed by its grandiose neighbours. There was something gallant about the little church – its survival in spite of everything development could throw at it. Once, that spire must have been a landmark. Now it was invisible to anyone who wasn't sitting, like me, on the rising ground of the central garden.

As I sat there I heard the first, distant bump of thunder – ominous, but also a promise of relief. The schoolgirls got up off the grass and wandered desultorily away, one of them still talking on her mobile. Their skirts barely covered their backsides, but then they barely had backsides, just endless legs. That, I reflected, would be Hannah in three or four years time. The little old lady was on the home straight, heading towards the gate by which I'd come in. I tried to imagine what it must be like not to be able to walk upright, to see only what lay within a metre or two of one's feet. And when one lay down, not to be able to gaze at the ceiling or the sky, but only at the end of the bed.

Now she'd gone, too, and there was only me and the gardener left. He'd finished his litter-circuit, and was in amongst the shrubs, loosening the drought-impacted soil with a hoe. Consideration of the old lady's plight had made me think about eye contact, how personal, even intimate, it was. If the gardener was to look up now and our eyes met, something else would have to happen as a consequence – a wave, a nod, some form of acknowledgement, no matter how microscopic. Alternatively, and what was more likely, we would look hastily away in embarrassment. It would be like accident-ally touching someone else in a swimming pool; the invisible veil of discretion and privacy would have been broken if only for a second.

That was why the girl was so disturbing. She stared, and her stare invaded and possessed me. She both assumed and im-posed a tyrannical intimacy. And there was that smell, too, which I had so far been unable to place, though I knew it so well ...

Where was she now? Next to me, here on the bench in this little garden? Behind me, with her hand resting lightly on my shoulder? I shuddered.

The sky was getting darker by the second now, and there was another rattle of thunder, closer and more protracted than the first. A couple of large, soft drops fell on the path in front of me leaving penny-sized patches. The gardener looked up at the heavens – a token gesture to let me, and anyone else who was looking, understand his reasons for knocking off – and then put the hoe back on the barrow and began trundling slowly away.

The drops were spattering down now, still so few and far between that you could hear the individual 'tap' as each one touched the leaves on its way down. It had turned weirdly, unseasonably dark. There was another, more purposeful crash of thunder, this time accompanied by a pale shimmer of lightning. Reluctantly I got up, but still didn't turn towards home. Instead, I walked towards the far end of the gardens, and went out of the gate and over the road to the church.

The building wasn't derelict; the fabric looked sound and the windows were intact.

But if there had ever been a churchyard it had long since been built over, and there were none of the usual boards and signs outside, naming the incumbent and advertising service times. Next to the door was a small plaque with the words 'The St Agnes Centre'.

I tried the door and it opened. Almost at once, the place was flooded with a hard white light from a cluster of spotlights high above the nave. I almost bumped into the switcher-on, a man with a shaven head, wearing an orange T-shirt and jeans.

'Let there be light – hey!' he cried, one hand to his chest in a gesture of exaggerated alarm. 'Never spotted you there.'

'Is it okay if I come in?' I asked.

'Let me see now...' he mused, finger to cheek. 'Yes, why not? The heavens are about to open unless I'm much mistaken, orphans of the storm welcome, we're not proud.'

I closed the door behind me. 'What happens here exactly?'

'Community art happens. Explanatory leaflet about the exhibition here, pamphlet about the building there. No charge, but please feel free to put something in the glass jar on your way out.'

'Thank you.'

The man bustled off to a partitioned office space in the corner and turned his attention to the computer screen. I picked up one of the leaflets. It said that 'Seasons of Life' was an exhibition of work by local artists, ranging from schoolchildren to old age pensioners, all of them amateurs. The other leaflet explained that St Agnes had been the parish church of this area until fifty years ago, when the parish had merged with its neighbour and the larger church had taken over. St Agnes had fallen into disuse until it had become the beneficiary of a millennium grant which had brought it back to life as an arts centre. According to the leaflet several of the church's more interesting features had been preserved, such as the 'hound window' on the north wall, and the font with its unusually detailed carved pedestal. The pews had all been removed, and the altar replaced by a sculpture of a thin, androgenous figure.

I decided I might as well have a look round. The storm was into its stride; bang overhead, the rain sounded like sustained machine gun fire against the cannon-boom of the thunder. Intermittent lightning made the spotlights falter. The curator, snug in his nook, appeared to be concentrating impassively on his work, but you could bet he was keeping an eye on his only customer. That was fine with me; it only took one other person for me to be safe.

Obeying the numbering, I began to the left of the door and moved round respectfully in a clockwise direction. There were some pictures on the walls, and others on easels, but most of the exhibits took the form of what you might broadly have termed sculptures – loose assemblages of stuff, put together to represent whatever it said on the card. Maybe I was too sceptical, but it didn't take a great artistic sensibility to place a bowl of apples, a sack of flour and a piece of honeycomb on a small table and call it 'Nature's Plenty'. Nor to scatter red and yellow paper leaves, along with nuts, on a rush mat, with the title 'Fall'. The graceless and deeply unoriginal thought 'Hannah could have done this' kept popping into my head. Also, there was something skewed about all this idealized rusticity in an urban setting. What was missing in the much-vaunted age-range were teenagers – the smart, cocky, disaffected young who might have injected some edge into these genteel proceedings.

Dutifully I moved round, past a photo-montage of babies, a collage of cereals and dried fruit, a collection of clay models and a plastic sand-box full of pebbles – I paused. Actually, I rather liked the box of pebbles. Especially because whoever had done it had given it a witty title: 'Young Sand'. The pebbles were in themselves beautiful: muted colours, black, white, veined and marbled, some speckled like eggs, others containing the spiralling whorls of fossils. The artist had trickled varnish over the stones so that some of them shone as if a wave had just splashed them. The item was no more complicated than any other, but it did what it was supposed to do – it had caught my attention and made me think, about time, and change.

As I stood there admiringly there was an especially loud clap of thunder and the lights went out. The contrast made it seem inky-black. My friend in the office let out a wail of anguish, followed by a brisk: 'Hang on, hang on, don't go away – I've got candles!'

In a minute he came out with a tray of nightlights and dotted them about the place. The effect was pleasing; almost all the exhibits benefited from being more softly illuminated.

He dusted off his palms. 'There we are. Signal for everything to come back on immediately.' He opened the door and peered out into the deluge. 'Not just us, then, the whole square's blacked out! I hope to God my report's still there, I'm not sure if I saved. '

He returned to the office and began talking on his mobile. I looked at the remaining exhibits, but nothing appealed to me as much as 'Young Sand'. The thunder moved on but it was still pouring with rain. I turned my attention to the church's special features as set out in the pamphlet. Weirdly, they too were in a rural vein. The eighteenth-century 'hound window' was exactly that – two dogs, one white, one brown, curled head to tail to form a circle. The font pedestal was much earlier if the guide was to be believed, and showed a cluster of tree trunks supporting the basin, with figures of animals and people just visible in between. I detected something wild and pantheistic in the carving – a suggestion of wilful sensuality and secrecy at odds with Christian baptism.

The rain was beginning to ease off and a pale, natural light illuminated the windows. I dropped a pound coin in the glass wine jar and called in the direction of the office: 'Very interesting – thanks.'

'You're welcome...' At that moment the

now-unnecessary lights came back on. 'Hooray!'

Near the door there was a damp patch on the ground, and for a moment I thought the rain might have come through the roof. But when I got closer I could see that this was no random leak. On the bleached pine boards were the prints of two small, bare feet, about half the size of my own, surrounded by a scattering of drops.

Patient as ever, she had been waiting for me.

I trudged back to Arbury Road, aching all over. The thought of turning out to fetch Hannah from after-school club was too much. As soon as I got in I rang Olwyn.

'Vicarage – Phil Owen here.'

'Phil, it's Fee.'

'Hallo! That was such a good evening. I must have enjoyed myself, I've been distinctly fragile all day.'

'Me too ... In fact I'm really not feeling well, I think I may be sickening...'

'Poor old you. Early bed.'

'I certainly intend ... Is Olwyn there?'

'She's not, she's doing her hunter-gatherer number at Tesco's.'

'When are you expecting her back?'

'She's only just gone – and it's Friday afternoon ... About this time tomorrow? Want me to pick up Hannah for you?'

'Oh God, Phil, I couldn't—'

'I'm going anyway, and God would be all in favour, I've done precious little else today to win His approval.'

'I'd be so, so grateful.'

'Save it, honestly. Doesn't she usually stay to after-school club? You might just give the school a bell and explain that I'll be coming – so they can let her know.'

'I will. Thanks, Phil, I owe you.'

I called the school and went to lie down in the bedroom. My eyes stung with tears of self-pity. I didn't deserve this, any of it – to feel so ill, and such a nervous wreck, to be plagued by supernatural visitations. Gimme a break, God! At least for once I was too tired and felt too lousy to lie awake fretting. Within five minutes I'd fallen into a shallow, churning sleep, in which I was plagued not so much by dreams but by fleeting, horrifying images of suffering and death – souls in torment, people screaming silently in an agony of mind and spirit, the devil leering and slavering over his wretched harvest. If God was up there, He was napping on the job, there was not the smallest hint of redemption, forgiveness, or peace. I was conscious of a dry mouth and aching joints and head, but could not even summon the energy to turn over or change my position. Least of all did I want to open my eyes. Who knew what I might see? Rigid and foetal I lay there, preferring the horrors in my head to those that haunted the real world.

I was eventually roused by Phil ringing the doorbell. I staggered along the corridor, pressed the buzzer and met them in the outer hall.

'Mum – you look awful,' said Hannah reprovingly.

'Have you said thank you to Phil?'

'Thank you for the lift.'

'Pleasure. Right, better scoot off, I left Meriel in the car. You get back to bed or wherever you were.'

'I really appreciate this.'

He dismissed this with a wave of the hand. 'We'll be in touch.'

Hannah was in the kitchen, helping herself out of the biscuit tin.

'Do you mind if I don't cook this evening, hon?' I asked. 'I just don't feel up to it.'

She shrugged. Signs of weakness in me had always embarrassed and irritated her.

'I think I'll lie down for a bit,' I said, as if I

hadn't already been doing that. 'See if I can shake it off.'

'Whatever.'

She went into the living room and turned on the television. It was an act of defiance. I remembered the schoolgirls in the park – what on earth would she be like when she was their age? When both of us were on form she was the best company in the world, but it didn't take much to rock the boat, and at the moment our craft felt distinctly frail and unseaworthy.

I returned to the bedroom, telling myself that all over the country, at this precise moment, nine year olds were eating biscuits and watching television, some of them entirely on their own. Hannah was very far from being neglected; there was no reason for me to beat myself up. I was a single parent for God's sake, I was entitled to an off-day every now and again.

I was just about to lie down on the bed when I felt a familiar sensation between my legs.

'Damn,' I muttered, but actually it was a comfort in a way to know that I'd come on. That, combined with the after-effects of a heavy night, explained why I felt so crap. Leaving my little companion aside – if only that were possible! – it appeared I wasn't going down with the flu, or in the early stages of a terminal illness.

I took a Tampax and clean knickers out of the drawer and went to the loo. As I sat down I could smell that smell – her smell – and thought *Oh no, not in here as well – is nothing sacred?* And then it dawned on me. I realized why that smell had always been so disturbingly familiar.

It was *my* smell, the most intimate of female odours, menstrual blood. The blood of the womb.

Fourteen

Later that night I called Phil. Olwyn answered the phone. It occurred to me that what with one thing and another she would have been perfectly justified in thinking I was making a play for her husband, but perhaps vicars' wives got used to these things, because she was her usual friendly, uninterfering self.

She shouted his name once, and then said: 'There's none so deaf – hang on a minute, Fee, I'll go and get him. He's just got back from a PCC meeting and probably thinks you're a bit of late Any Other Business and has adopted avoidance mode.'

As I sat there waiting, I reflected that, in a sense, Any Other Business was exactly what I was.

'Fee.'

'Phil, this is going to seem impertinent.'

'I very much doubt it.'

'The thing is – well, any port in a storm. My belief, such as it is, may not be worth a hill of beans, but yours is.'

'Actually, anyone's is good. We're all equal in the sight of God. But I hear what you're saying. You'd like me to intercede on your behalf.'

'Please.'

'Then I shall.'

I closed my eyes in a moment's gratitude, and screwed up my courage for the next embarrassing question.

'Do I have to be there?'

He replied, through a laugh: 'No. This is prayer, not a seance. Or, incidentally an exorcism.'

'I understand that.'

'On the other hand if you want to add your voice to the proceedings it would do no harm and it might do some good.'

'Okay,' I said. 'Your place or mine?'

'God's place.'

Talk about a sign of the times. Till recently I'd scarcely been near a church since my schooldays, but this would make it the third time this year if one counted the St Agnes Centre. After all, I hadn't known it was an arts centre when I crossed the road to go in. I had wanted what only consecrated ground could give – sanctuary.

It was a Saturday afternoon, so I left Hannah with Meriel. Olwyn announced that she was going to watch Wimbledon.

'Do you play?' she asked.

'Not since school, and not very well even then.'

'Only we're always looking for other not-too-serious people for a bit of social tennis.'

'Go on Mum,' said Hannah. 'You'd be good.'

She had no grounds whatever for this optimism, but somehow it was agreed that I'd give it a go some time. Then Phil and I walked the twenty yards or so to St Mary's. It was nothing to look at, a serviceable

Edwardian red-brick pile, with none of St Agnes's ancient beauty. But inside, it was a different story. This was a real place of worship, warm and cared-for, full of the scent of polish and flowers, with a children's corner, a notice board, embroidered kneelers, an urn on a trestle table at the back, and an electronic keyboard as well as an organ with sheaves of music propped on the stand. There was only one stained-glass window, over the altar, depicting a calm-faced Jesus of the Burne-Jones style, firm but fair, like a hippyish schoolmaster.

'I suggest we use the transept,' said Phil. 'It's easier to get a focus in the smaller space.'

'You know best.'

'We'll see.' He led the way into the side chapel. Here there were a dozen folding chairs and a white-clothed table with a plain wooden cross.

'I'd say take a pew, but ... Anyway, sit down.'

I perched on one of the chairs in the front row and he pulled another round so that he was at right angles; between me and the crucifix.

'We'll begin by putting ourselves and our difficulties in God's hands.'

He leaned forward, clasped his own hands loosely between his knees, and closed his eyes. Since this was all taking place at my instigation, and I had elected to be here, I somewhat self-consciously did the same. Phil waited a moment and then spoke.

'Oh Lord, we ask that You will be with us as we ask for help. Watch over us and guide us. Give us wisdom in our decisions, and serenity and tolerance in our dealings. Make us calm, generous, and unafraid. For Your name's sake. Amen.'

'Amen,' I muttered.

In spite of myself I was affected. Wisdom, serenity, tolerance ... Bring them on! Calm, generous, unafraid ... Please, oh please, let me be those things! It was strange, but soothing, to have these powerful representations made on my behalf. I wondered if there was a standard form of words for occasions like this, and if so whether he had used it, or simply made things up as he went along.

'Right.' He straightened up and slapped both hands on his legs in a down-to-business gesture. 'Let's try and be quite clear what it is we're asking for.'

'I suppose...' I hesitated, conscious of a

heavy responsibility to make good use of this opportunity. 'If I'm honest—'

'You must certainly be that.'

'I'm scared shi– stiff, a lot of the time. I don't know what's going on, or why. I don't know who the girl is, or when I'm going to see her. I mean—' I spread my arms and looked around – 'she's probably here now.'

'So you would like *not* to see her. Not to be scared.'

I shrugged helplessly. 'Yes.' It sounded so lame, so feeble.

'But you need an explanation, too.'

'Yes. And also – she wants something from me, so *badly*. And I don't know what. She wants help, but I'm helpless, in every sense. Talk about a no-win situation.'

'That may be true,' said Phil, 'but then we're not looking to win. Resolution is what we're after. Reconciliation. Closure. Yes?'

'Yes.'

'Then that's what we'll ask for.' He was matter of fact, he made it sound, if not easy, at least simple. I suppose if one is in constant touch with a Higher Authority you're more relaxed about these things.

'As long as you understand,' he went on, 'that there will be no miracle, in the obvious sense. You won't have an answer to every-

215

thing right away.'

'Of course not.' I wanted to remind him that I was agnostic, trying any port in a storm – that it was he who truly believed this might do some good.

'Let's pray,' he said.

Once again we clasped our hands and bowed our heads. As we did so I heard the main door of the church open and close as someone came in.

'Dear Lord, we ask You again to bear us company and be in our hearts, and in our heads, as we pray. We've come together here to ask that Fee should be free from fear, and that she be granted understanding of those things that have made her afraid in recent weeks. Whatever needs to be done to bring peace to herself and to the girl that she sees, please give her, and all of us, the strength and the opportunity to do it. Grant insight and patience to all those in whom she confides her fears. Above all else, Lord, let us do right, by others and ourselves, and help us to know that life is good. Bless Fee, Hannah, and all who love them in this world and the next. For Your name's sake...'

'Amen.' We said it together this time, and remained still for a moment, in silence. When I did open my eyes I blinked slightly as if waking.

'That's it,' said Phil. 'We're in His hands.'

I remembered again the saying about faith being both belief and trust. In fact there was no doubt I did feel calmer, but that could simply have been due to the circumstances. As we left the transept I saw a woman – presumably the one who had come in a moment ago – setting up music stands near the keyboard, and at the same time another woman ushered three children, carrying instruments, through the main door. One of the children was dark, and my skin prickled until she turned round and I saw it wasn't her.

'The St Mary's Metronomes,' explained Phil. 'Morning. They're our band for the family service.' He glanced at me. 'You and Hannah are always welcome.'

'I don't know...'

He smiled. 'Don't worry, it's not a trade-off. Our prayers hold good even if I never see you again.' He opened the door. 'On the other hand we're hoping you and Mark will come and have supper with us soon.'

'Thanks. And thank you for everything.'

He placed his hand on my shoulder, firmly – conferring a blessing. 'All will be well.'

★　★　★

Buoyed up by all this unaccustomed spiritual activity, I took Hannah to New Look and bought her a distinctly ungodly pink T-shirt with *Girls Rule!* in spangly writing across the chest. She was over the moon. I had bought myself a quiet evening.

Or so I thought. As we walked up Arbury Road I noticed an unfamiliar flash dark blue jeep drawn up outside our flat in a residents' parking bay. The driver was sitting behind the wheel, so he was almost certainly not a resident, and ready to take off at the first sign of a traffic warden. I was in the act of taking out my key, when I heard the jeep door clunk shut, and footsteps came up behind me. Even in broad daylight, right outside my own front door all my London programming kicked in and I gripped the key tight, point outwards between my fingers, as I turned round.

'Surprise, surprise – hi there.'

'Dean!'

'Hello Fee. Hey, princess, look at you!'

'Hannah, this is your Dad. Remember?' I added, with bitter sarcasm.

'Hello.'

I could hear the uncertainty in Hannah's voice, and see it on her face, and reproached myself. I was reeling, but for her sake it was important I strike the right tone.

'Come in – but move that thing first, they hunt in packs round here.'

'Don't you have a guest thingy? Lots of people do?'

'I'm afraid not.' With difficulty I restrained myself from saying that not only did I not have a guest thingy, I didn't have a car.

'No problem, I'll be back in a tick—' He paused and looked down at Hannah. 'Want to jump in while I park her?'

She glanced up at me. 'Is that okay?'

'Of course, go on. Dean, I have to shut this after me, but when you come back, just ring 1A.'

'Gotcher.'

God, he hadn't changed, I thought, as I went into the flat. Not many people these days used the term 'gotcher' without a hint of irony, but Dean was one of them. He was big, handsome, genial, blokey – and a bit of a buffoon. A stranger to the things of the mind. I was prepared to bet that he was congratulating himself on this act of fatherly spontaneity, turning up on our doorstep unannounced, probably bearing gifts and promises, the years of absence and neglect completely forgotten. If he'd ever thought about them at all, which I doubted.

In the living room I glanced round. How would our home – his daughter's home – strike him? Not that Dean, if memory served, was someone who expended much interest or effort on his environment. I decided it all looked all right: homely and welcoming, the mark on the wall almost invisible.

I opened the window. The fierce heatwave had passed and it was a pleasant, overcast day with temperatures at the seasonal average. I couldn't see Dean, Hannah, or the jeep. For a fleeting moment I had visions of kidnap, 'tug of love father snatches daughter' – what had I done? But then I reminded myself that the last thing Dean wanted, now or ever, was responsibility for his child, and as I did so they reappeared, crossing the street, and I darted back in and went to buzz the door open for them.

'Hey!' he exclaimed as he came in, 'this is really nice. Hannah, you going to give me the guided tour?'

'Tea or something stronger?' I asked.

'Got a beer?'

'Not cold I'm afraid.'

'That'll do.'

'Okay,' said Hannah, 'Well—' she flapped

her arms – 'this is the kitchen as you can see.'

'Kitchen. Yup, brilliant...'

She towed him away. It was surreal. I heard her piping commentary and his exclamations of approval. They appeared in the bedroom and Hannah pointed up at the skylight. Dean, nodding, looked up dutifully, and then picked her up and hugged her, twirling her round and planting smacking kisses on her face. He didn't realize he could be seen – not that embracing his own daughter was a crime – but Hannah did, and looked rather self-conscious. That's my girl, I thought.

'In here,' I said as they came back down the corridor. Hannah appeared shortly after Dean, proudly wearing her new top. She had put her hair up in a glittery scrunchy. It was clear that everything they said about little girls flirting with their fathers was true. I sent her to bring crisps from the kitchen, and handed Dean his Carlsberg.

'Great. Cheers.' He sat down, keeping to the edge of the chair. It was not so much that he appeared tense, or anxious – he was simply signalling that he would not be staying long.

That was fine with me. 'How did you know

where to find us?' I asked, as pleasantly as I could.

'I called your old dot,' he said – by this he meant Julia – 'and she told me.'

'Right...' I made a mental note to have a word with my mother about this at the first opportunity. 'So tell us what you've been up to.'

He was doing well, apparently, as area manager of a well-known electronics chain. Way back when we had been together, he had affected a vaguely rock-and-roll approach to life, but now I could see that the seeds of bourgeois respectability had been there all along. He'd run a sandwich bar, for Christ's sake! And deep down he'd always been more materialistic than me. He liked stuff – and now he was beginning to accumulate it, starting with the fancy jeep.

Hannah returned with the crisps – 'Thanks, sweetheart' – and sat down by me on the sofa. But though she was next to me, she had eyes for no-one but Dean. She was plainly enchanted; I was baffled, not by her enchantment which was understandable enough, but by our past history. How had I ever found this man sexy? What had been different about him, or me, that had lighted the blue touch paper of passion? I could neither remember nor imagine it. I was indifferent, to the point where I could scarcely summon a smidgin of appropriate resentment.

'...out Ealing way,' he said, 'with a decent garden.' He was describing his house. Something occurred to me.

'Does anyone live there with you?' I shouldn't have asked this in front of Hannah, but I was eaten up with curiosity.

'Oh, no,' he replied cheerily. 'On my tod, just the way I like it.' He seemed to consider this, and must have found it wanting, because he added, 'For the moment. You know.'

'Sounds marvellous,' I said thinly. 'I'm hoping to buy somewhere in the spring.'

'You should Fee, you really should. Come and look out my way while you're about it. I can really recommend it as an area. Lots of green, good schools—'

I wasn't going to listen to advice on education from Dean, the holder of one GCSE in technical drawing. 'The school Hannah goes to at the moment is excellent.'

'Great! You like school, do you?'

'It's okay,' said Hannah. It wasn't quite the ringing endorsement I'd hoped for, but fortunately he laughed.

'You'll be glad one day, princess.'

'Is it okay if I go on the computer?'

'Of course,' I said, 'off you go.'

Dean watched her fondly. 'She's gorgeous. She's got your eyes, Fee.'

I would have dismissed this as a nauseating cliché, except that it was true.

'Dean—'

'Fee—'

We'd both spoken at once, but it was Dean who continued.

'—I know it's been a long time, much too long, and of course you're entitled to say no, but I wondered if Hannah would like to come and spend part of the summer holidays with me. I've got some extra time due, and I'm not going abroad till September. What do you reckon?'

I believe I gawped. He was unbelievable. 'You'd have to ask her.'

'I know, I realize, yeah...' He fidgeted, and rolled his glass between his palms, for the first time looking slightly discomforted. 'But before I do that I want to know if it's okay with you.'

I was perched uncomfortably on the horns of a dilemma. Dean had a fucking nerve, swanning in here after how many years? Gagging to distribute largesse to the poor womenfolk, showing off to Hannah, trying to buy her affection – he could get stuffed! But the fact remained that I badly needed more cover for the school summer holidays. Moral outrage warred with expediency in my breast.

'I realize I can't rock up here and expect you to make your mind up right away, just like that,' he said.

'Damn right.'

'I was thinking all the way over, what if she tells me to sod off and slams the door in my face? You'd be entitled, I do realize that.'

'Glad to hear it.'

'On the other hand I thought, nothing ventured nothing gained, better late than never.'

The platitudes were coming thick and fast. 'Two wrongs don't make a right,' I said, but sarcasm was wasted on Dean.

'Exactly! I'm pleased you see it like that, too.'

We sat there, on either side of the abyss. 'You'll want some time to think about it, yeah?'

'No,' I said, 'I can tell you right now, Hannah's not going anywhere till I see where she's going, and what she's going to.'

Dean looked mightily relieved. 'Of course,

no question! The two of you must come out and see the house, I was thinking of arranging it so she had her own special bedroom, there are three, so—'

'Hang on. Dean, nothing's agreed. It's years since we saw you, Hannah doesn't know you – I hardly know you myself.'

'Come on, Fee, we go back a long way. You and I have history.'

'We certainly do,' I said acidly, 'which is why you're going to have to work your butt off for the privilege of seeing your daughter.'

'I suppose.' For a man who just a moment ago had been only too anxious to assume the mantle of prodigal father, he was quite comically crestfallen. In my heart of hearts I knew Hannah would be perfectly safe – and certainly indulged – *chez* Dean, but that wasn't the point. He could fucking well jump through a few hoops first.

'For instance,' I said. 'There may be no-one living with you, but I don't suppose you've been living like a monk.'

'Well, no, I've got a lady friend, obviously.'

'Obviously. I'm telling you here and now, Dean, that *if* – and it's a humungous if – *if* Hannah were to stay a few days at your place I don't want there to be the smallest whiff of the lady friend. Not so much as a toothbrush. Not a single aromatherapy candle or an artificial sweetener—'

'Steady on, I use those!'

So deep-fried-Mars-bar man had had a dietary road to Damascus. 'I don't care, Dean. I don't want Hannah meeting this woman, or the next one, or any of the ones before. Got that?'

'What if Nicky and I get married?'

'Then I'll eat my hat, and Hannah can be a bridesmaid.'

Dean poured the remains of the Carlsberg into his glass, drained it and put the glass down.

'So when would the two of you like to come out and visit?'

'Let's see...' I fetched my bag and got out my diary. It was such fun making him squirm. 'Saturday week. We'll come for lunch.'

I could see a whole raft of nervous considerations flitting through his mind – shopping, beers with mates, his squash game, the match on TV. But I didn't give a stuff what he usually did on a Saturday, if he was thinking of having Hannah to stay he was going to have to put her first.

'All right?' I asked.

'Terrific.' He shook his head as he said

this, an intriguing double message. 'I'll look forward to it. Tell you what, let me give you my card, then you can get in touch any time.'

He took his wallet from the back pocket of his trousers and removed a business card, on which were a rake of numbers and addresses beneath the words: *Dean Files, Area Manager, Business Solutions, South Eastern Region.*

'Thanks.' I gave the card only the most peremptory glance, and put it in my bag, but I remained standing, giving the heaviest possible hint to Dean that it was time to leave.

Instead of which, annoyingly, he leaned back in his chair, leaving me looking slightly foolish.

'So how are you, Fee?'

'Fine.'

'You're looking great.'

I kept my mouth shut. To say anything would be to give Dean the impression that I gave a damn about his opinion.

'You asked me so I'll ask you – anyone in your life?'

It was true, I had asked him, but only because it was relevant to the discussion, not because I was interested.

'That's none of your business,' I said, and

immediately wished I hadn't. A simple 'no' would have been both more dignified and less contentious. He held up one palm in a gesture of dignified acceptance which I found infuriating.

'Right – you're dead right.'

'Dean—'

'Better dash, I was supposed to be some-where—' he glanced at his watch as he rose – 'half an hour ago, but this was more im-portant. I'll just say good-bye to Hannah, down here is she...?'

He was probably hoping for a nice little private farewell, but he'd reckoned without Hannah's programming. I'd taught her it was good manners to see guests off at the door, so no sooner had he got there than he was following her back down the corridor.

'So,' he said, 'you're coming to see me next Saturday.'

'Am I?'

'Saturday week,' I corrected. I didn't want any misunderstandings that might enable him to wriggle out of it.

'That's the one.'

'Cool.' Hannah looked at me. 'Are you coming?'

I was by no means sure which answer was wanted, or expected, but there was only one

I was prepared to give.

'Oh yes,' I said, 'don't you worry. I'm coming.'

One benefit arising from Dean's visit was that I had an undisturbed evening. Or to put it another way, if there were any disturbances I was too put about to notice them. I rang my mother and told her he'd been round, making it as clear as politeness would allow that I had not appreciated her role in the matter. It was water off a duck's back, she was too taken up with wedding preparations, and in her current frame of mind any interest shown in us by Dean was to be filed under 'A Good Thing'. I was wasting my time.

When I went along to bed, Hannah was still awake. As I took out the bookmark and began to read, her voice came from behind the screen:

'Do you think he's nice?'

I had the impression she was being careful how she phrased this question. It was neutral, open-ended – it gave nothing away about her own opinion. I wondered if she'd picked up anything of our conversation when she was on the computer, and if so what she'd made of it. She had extremely sensitive antennae for these things.

'He seems nice, doesn't he?' I replied, keeping it chatty and non-committal.

'Yes.' There was a pause, then she appeared round the screen. 'But Mum—'

'Come,' I beckoned her over, and put my arm round her. 'What?'

'Do *you* like him?'

Poor Hannah, she was on the rack. She wanted everything to be okay – her and Dean, Dean and me, the three of us. Most of all, her and me: she didn't want to do anything that would hurt or offend me. I loved and respected my daughter more than she would ever know.

But for this reason she deserved more than flannel. Honesty, I considered, was more important than mere comfort.

'I *really* liked him once,' I said, 'but then I stopped. After all, he left us a long time ago. But I don't think he's a wicked person, far from it. And I think he's sorry, and really wants to be friends, with you especially. So shall we give it a go?'

Hannah nodded. 'Let's give it a go.'

She went back to bed. I don't know how quickly she went to sleep, but she remained quiet. I read for a little while, and then turned the light out. After the overcast day it had turned into a clear night, I could even make out one or two stars beyond the smeary glass. The room felt peaceful.

My last thought before dropping off was that of course I had been attributing too much to Dean. It wasn't Dean who had banished the horrors.

There was every possibility that I was witnessing the power of prayer.

Fifteen

Various phrases spring to mind: 'the darkest hour is just before dawn' ... 'the calm before the storm' ... The remark beloved of cowboys in Indian country: 'It's quiet ... too quiet.' At any rate, though I didn't know it at the time, the period following my visit to Phil, and Dean's to us, was a hiatus – the slightly ominous lull that so often precedes all hell breaking out.

Of course it would have been astoundingly unlikely if the girl had simply disappeared as a result of Phil's intercessions. He had stated categorically: there would be no miracle. But such was the power of auto-suggestion that after a few days I began cautiously to congratulate myself: I had taken steps, and they had proved successful.

Ironically, it was during this peaceful interlude that Mark and I had our first falling-out. I suppose we had to some time, the romantic phase can't last for ever, and this was a sign of our relationship growing up. The reason for it was an odd one, though.

It began one evening when he was round at my place, and Hannah was at my mother's. He passed a perfectly casual – and flattering – comment on my appearance.

'You're looking fantastic these days,' was what he said, and I – knowing I was doing it but unable to stop myself – did that classic female thing of assuming an unfavourable, retrospective comparison.

'How was I looking before, then?'

'Come on, Fee.'

'I was only asking.'

'Well, forgive me if I'm wrong, but you were ill that time at my place, and you've been preoccupied ... I've no idea why, it's none of my business. But it's great to see you looking better. Looking yourself, should I say.'

I should have been pleased that he noticed these things, but there was something in his manner that I found irritating. He was being presumptuous. Looking 'myself'? And what was that, exactly? If I didn't know, how on earth could he?

'I've had a lot on my mind,' I said, sniffily.

We were sitting at the table in my flat, having had supper. He gazed intently at me, his eyes moving from one to the other of mine. 'Want to share it, as they say?'

This whole evening was a big step, the first time he'd spent time here, and met Hannah properly. If ever there was a time to keep things calm and harmonious, this was it. But suddenly I was on my high horse. While I had secrets from him, things that I kept to myself, I still had a modicum of control. Also, I was afraid that if I told him everything that had been going on, it was perfectly possible he'd file me under 'barking' and back off.

'Hmm? Fee?' He leaned back in his chair, his wine glass resting against his chest. 'Say something, if it's only sod off.'

'Okay,' I said. 'But I insist you keep an open mind.'

'Is there any other kind?'

We were about to find out. He listened

every bit as attentively as Phil, but I could sense a difference. Whereas Phil's silence had been neutral, absorbent as a sponge, Mark's seemed to me in my touchy state to be freighted with thought: suppositions, hypotheses, calculations – arguments-in-waiting.

I ended with my visit to Phil, and the prayers in his church. After all, I was still hoping that that *was* the end.

'Since then,' I said, 'for whatever reason, everything's been quiet.'

'And you attribute this improvement to the power of prayer?'

I saw a glimpse of his business manner, and I didn't care for it.

'Not necessarily. But you have to admit it's a coincidence.'

'May I say something?' he asked. In my experience when people say that they mean they're going to say it anyway, but that you won't like it. I was right, because when I didn't answer he went on regardless.

'I wouldn't dream of implying that what's happened was in your imagination, that it had no objective reality. Reality is relative after all—'

'Struth!'

'It's a question of perception, we each have

our own. But I think it would be a bad mistake for you, who on your own admission have no religious belief, to convince yourself you've undergone some Damascene conversion—'

'*What?*'

'—when really it's been more like self help. You're an intelligent woman—'

'Gee, thanks.'

'—and you found ways and means. Which is good. Great, in fact. But you're the one who did it. You should be pleased with yourself, not grateful to God.' He gave a cold, careless little laugh. 'Let alone your vicar friend.'

That was when I detected the glint of rancour beneath the rational argument. Was this whole exchange about testosterone, then?

Now it was my turn to be cool. 'Phil was the conduit,' I said. 'He put the offer on the table, and when I didn't know what else to do, I picked it up.'

'You never mentioned any of this to me.'

'Why should I?'

'I'd have thought that was obvious.'

'Not to me. And anyway I didn't want to bore you with it.'

'You could have let me be the judge of

whether or not it was boring.'

'I'm sorry,' I said, wholly unapologetically. But he wasn't interested anyway, the only voice he was listening to now was his own.

'Tell me,' he said frostily, 'is this what all the trouble was about at my place – the first time you came over?'

'Yes.'

'But even then, in my flat, after – you didn't think to tell me – to confide in me?'

'Mark, I—'

'I must say I find it extraordinary.' He was being pompous. The most unaffected man I'd ever met (so I thought), and he was being unconscionably pompous – I could taste the sourness of disappointment in my mouth.

'For Christ's sake, Mark, I've said I'm sorry, what do you want, blood?'

'A little honesty wouldn't go amiss.'

That did it. 'Honesty? If we're talking fucking honesty here, why don't you take a long, hard look in the mirror? This isn't about me, or what I did or didn't say, this is about your poxy male ego! You're as jealous as hell because I confided in another man – a happily married man, by the way, but I wouldn't expect you to know about that – and he sorted it!'

I knew at once that I'd gone too far. It was

that bit about the happily married man. Mark's face was pinched and white, he seemed to get smaller before my eyes. Then he got up and walked out, of the flat.

Two doors banged shut behind him.

Hannah appeared in the doorway. 'What's the matter?'

'Nothing.'

She looked round. 'Where's he gone?'

'He had to dash off—' I came up with the first thing I could think of that would make sense to her – 'to collect Reuben.'

'Oh!' She pulled a face, turned to go, and then turned back again with an expression of consternation. 'He's not bringing him back here, is he?'

'Good heavens, no!' I got up, gave her a hug and ushered her back along the corridor. 'No, no. That's it, he's gone.'

Two days after that was the Saturday that Hannah and I were going to visit Dean, and I still hadn't spoken to Mark when we left. This lent an extra piquancy to the expedition, as though I were doing it to spite him, though nothing could have been further from the truth.

Hannah's happy excitement only underlined my own gloom, though God knows I tried to enter into the spirit of the thing.

'How long will it take?'

'Once we're on the tube – about forty-five minutes.'

'Do we have to change?'

'Just once.'

'Will he meet us?' Whether from tact or shyness, she still never used 'Dad'. Dean was always 'he'.

'He won't have to, his house isn't far.'

'Are you sure you know where it is?'

'Hannah – I've got the A to Z.'

'I hope it's nice, so I can go and stay.'

I made some amiable, non-committal sound, and Hannah didn't push it. For such a feisty child she could be wonderfully diplomatic. After we'd changed trains and were on the final leg on the Central Line, she rested her head on my shoulder for a minute, as if assuring me of her loyalty. I was reminded how much I dreaded losing her, and how strongly I must resist the temptation to be clinging or possessive. My daughter must go out into the world with her head high and her shoulders back, ready to take it on with confidence and courage. Like her mother.

Yeah, right! As Hannah would have said.

I had to admit, grudgingly, that Dean's house *was* nice. The décor was plain, comfortable, bachelor-chic, but not stark. The living room had a whole wall of music, and speakers in every room; not many books, but you couldn't have everything. The kitchen was white and modern but showed every sign of being used – there were even apples on a hand-painted plate on the side, though that might have been to impress me.

Upstairs, his bedroom was in denim blue and white, with curtains hanging from outsize wooden rings and bed linen in mattress-ticking stripes. It had its own en-suite shower, no bigger than a cupboard, but enough to impress Hannah. There was no sign whatever – I checked – of female occupancy.

Of the two other bedrooms, the smallest housed Dean's computer, and a sofa-bed. The other, which overlooked the garden, was the one he said Hannah could sleep in if she came, but he'd had the good sense not to attempt to trick it out in a one-size-fits-all girlie style. It was simple and fresh, with cream walls and white bedding, a white louvre blind and a wheat-coloured carpet in a nubbly, hard-wearing texture. The one splash of colour was a vase of flowers, one of those mixed bunches you can buy at filling stations. He was trying.

The main bathroom was enormous – converted from the smaller original one and the fourth bedroom – with a trendy freestanding bathtub and a shower three people could have used together without touching; though I was pretty sure that was not what Dean had had in mind. He'd let rip a bit in here, with mirror tiles, plants, a peacock chair and a wicker trolley groaning with metro-manly products.

Hannah was entranced. 'Wow...!'

'My pride and joy,' said Dean. 'I always wanted a nice bathroom.'

That was the first I'd heard of this particular ambition, and I couldn't resist saying waspishly: 'Me too.'

Hannah parted the slats of the blind and peered out. 'Can we see the garden?'

'Sure.'

The garden was nothing special, a large rectangle of grass – with the tufty appearance of the infrequently but recently mown – with a strip of paving nearest the house and a tree at the far end. I entertained a fleeting image of Mark's beautiful, secret bower and my heart lurched.

'Haven't done much with this,' said Dean, striding to the centre of the lawn and kicking at the grass speculatively with his toe. 'Gardening's not really my thing.'

'You could have a trampoline,' suggested Hannah.

'Good idea.' Dean slapped his midriff. 'Bit of bouncing, do me good...'

She smiled.

We went to a nearby pub for lunch. Dean drove us in the jeep, with Westlife – the crawler! – on the CD player.

'Do you like these guys?' he asked Hannah.

'They're okay.'

'Who's your favourite at the moment?'

'The Mechanicals.'

'Blimey, shows what I know.' Dean craned his neck to catch my eye in the rearview mirror. 'Ever heard of them?'

'Oh yes. They're much edgier than this lot.'

He laughed, slapping the wheel with both hands. 'Face it, Bambi would be edgier than these lads!'

Hannah laughed out loud at this. He was doing everything right, damn him.

The area we drove through was leafy and pleasant – a much more family-friendly neighbourhood than the one where we lived. At the pub, Dean had booked a table in the garden. There was a children's corner with a slide, and a run with rabbits and guinea pigs – Hannah was not yet too cool and grown-up for these things, and while we were waiting for the food she took her bottle of coke and joined another girl on the grass, cooing over the cuddly rodents.

'I've missed a lot,' said Dean fondly.

'Yup.'

He shook his head. 'She's such a great girl ... She's a credit to you, Fee.'

'I was lucky.'

'Don't run yourself down.'

'Just being realistic.'

There was a silence while we gazed at our daughter. Then I felt his eyes come back to me.

'So what do you think?' he asked eagerly.

'About what?'

'You know – about Hannah spending some time here in the holidays.'

'She's never stayed anywhere on her own, except my mother's. She'd have to come for the day first, and see how that goes.'

Under the pretence of common sense and caution, I was being mildly obstructive, and we both knew it. I could see no possible objection to Hannah spending time with this keen, straightforward, indulgent, pleasantly vain man – no objection, that is, apart from my own bitterness over the past. But the bitterness was there, and would have what was due to it.

'All right, fair dos.' I was sure Dean was used to getting his own way, and was exerting superhuman self-control. 'Let's do that then.'

He transferred his gaze back to Hannah. Did he, I wondered, have any idea what it would be like to have our daughter's company for a couple of days, let alone a week? Had he thought of the lack of privacy, the constant threat of boredom – his own and hers – the catering, the curtailment of his freedom? She had no friends out here, he would be the sole source of company, entertainment, food...

'I'll need some tips,' he said, as if reading my mind. 'I'm a beginner – nobody's fault but mine.'

He offered us a lift home, but I declined in the face of Hannah's moaning and pleading. I'd had quite enough of Dean's wonderfulness for one day, but the price I paid was Hannah's shut, resentful face all the way home.

Sitting on the tube with no newspaper, and no conversation forthcoming, I checked my mobile for messages. There was a text from Mark: *I'm sorry R U? Pls advise so nmal svice cn b resumed.*

When I first read it my heart leapt – everything was fine! Then I did that thing of re-reading the few words over and over again, in a variety of different lights until I was no longer sure what they meant, or how I should take them. Okay, he *said* he was sorry, but wasn't he being a bit glib? Just when I needed understanding he had been high-handed and obnoxious. And what did I have to be sorry for? Then, of course, I remembered, and the memory made me wince. But the problem still remained. He had *not* understood, and that was unlikely to change. I put the phone away.

That night, she was back. I was aware of the heavy silence that always accompanied her, enclosing me, cutting me off. The atmosphere in the living room grew thick with her presence and her smell. I felt, quite distinctly as I sat on the sofa, a soft pressure against my side, and a light, damp touch on my cheek.

I was frightened to move, and risk the effects of disturbing her. When I did finally summon the courage to get up and go to bed, I saw her standing by the wall. And for the first time she began to raise her right arm, the hand palm uppermost. With a sob, I closed the door. Far from being banished, she had drawn closer, and with her what I feared most – the possibility that she was part of me.

Trembling in bed, I got out my mobile, re-read Mark's message and texted back at once, before I had time to change my mind. *Yes.*

Sixteen

It appeared that far from being banished, she was coming closer all the time. Through my terror I had a sense of impending resolution, or crisis. Whatever it was she wanted, that I needed to understand, was terribly near now: no further than the next room. I was much too afraid to take any initiative, to hold out my hand to her as she had held out hers to me, but I remembered Phil saying, 'We're in His hands now,' and took some comfort in the passive trust this imp ied.

I was confused, weak and scared But I could only wait.

Thank God also, that there were plenty of practicalities to attend to, and I hurled myself in them. We were busy at work. Dean and I had agreed that Hannah would spend the following Saturday with him. I'd take her out there on the tube, he would bring her back by eight o'clock that evening. The arrangement suited me because it was the weekend before my mother's wedding, and I was due to visit her, in order to show an appropriate filial interest in the occasion.

When Dean had been conspicuous by his absence I had been angry, but also smugly superior, the plucky little woman coping alone. Now he was back, bearing gifts and enticements and I was insanely jealous. What I wanted was for him to stay away, leave Hannah and her affections strictly alone, and give us money – the everyday maintenance that was our due and his duty. I had never enlisted the dubious assistance of the CSA, reckoning that it would involve too much hassle and I'd rather go it alone. Now I was furious with myself for not having at once exacted our rights, and instead allowing him to play the gel-haired, jeep-driving, iPod-toting Santa Claus.

When I arrived at my mother's, she got her retaliation in first.

'So how did it go with Dean?'

'Hannah was bowled over, predictably enough.'

'Splendid, that's the main thing...' She gave me a sidelong look. 'Isn't it?'

'Julia, you really shouldn't have dished out our address and number to him without consulting me. There was no time for me to get my head together – we were bounced, and I don't like being bounced.'

She shook her head, but not in sorrow. 'I must say, Fee, I think you're being over-sensitive. The man's back, he's not a monster and he wants to help out – make the most of it.'

I had almost forgotten how obsessed she was with surface; an appearance of ease and harmony and respectability. The maintenance of a brave face and a good show had seen her through the exigencies of her extraordinary marriage, so why shouldn't it work in other, lesser situations?

Anyway, there was no point in pursuing the matter, particularly not today when we were scheduled to be doing our mother/daughter thing.

'Come up and see what I'm wearing,' she said.

It was a sleek shift with a cropped double-breasted jacket, in pale green shantung. The jacket had a stand-up collar and big buttons in the Jackie Kennedy style, and there was an embroidered pill-box hat with a little veil to match. I told her, truthfully, that she would look stunning in it.

She held it against her and surveyed her reflection. 'I do hope so ... It's hard at my age to find something suitably festive, but which will also see me out, as they say. What about you, have you and Hannah hit the shops?'

'No – we'll go this week.'

'I hope you haven't left it too late.'

'Julia, we've got a whole week!'

'But there's school—'

'We'll go after school. Every day if necessary.'

'I suppose so. Personally, I just hate to shop under pressure.'

'There won't be any pressure,' I lied. 'We shall enjoy it. And,' I added pointedly, 'we won't let you down.'

That was a low blow, which my mother very properly ignored. Once the wedding outfit was back in its plastic bag she opened a drawer and took out a dog-eared A4 envelope, handing it to me with a smile.

'I've been having a clear-out,' she said, 'and look what I found – some old photographs I forgot to put in albums. Bring them down and take a look, it's nearly glass of wine time.'

I sat on the sofa with my glass of Sauvignon and a dish of roasted cashews on the table next to me, and my mother on the other side, close enough to give a commentary but not actually touching – a nice metaphor for our relationship.

The photos were a mixed bag, each one popping up at me with the mixture of recognition and shock, the twisted reality of a dream. There were a few of my parents' wedding: Julia long-legged and panda-eyed with her thick silky hair falling to her shoulders from beneath her floppy hat; my father in a white suit, paisley shirt and Beatle-bangs. They looked so perfect, and beautiful, the *jeunesse dorée* of their day. When had the trouble started? When had their groovy kind of love turned into a horrible, secret hell?

My mother, peering at these, smiled and shook her head. 'Heavens, what do we look like?'

'You look great,' I said. But the words tasted bad in my mouth.

There were some of me, with them and on my own: on beaches, in the garden, at assorted birthday parties, wearing fancy dress. I was on much safer ground here. My mother had never been able to sew, but she had a genius for witty ideas that could be realized without the aid of needle and thread.

'Rapunzel!' I exclaimed. 'I remember those big itchy plaits.'

'You won second prize in that outfit. It was extremely effective, though I shouldn't say it.'

'Half a hundredweight of yellow double-knitting wool and the prize was in the bag.'

'And the wimple,' she reminded me. 'Don't forget that – a tribute to my skill with cardboard and stapler.'

At the bottom of the pile there were a sheaf of those professionally taken school photos, framed in brown card: three of me at various stages of primary-school development – gap in the teeth and fringe; big teeth and hairslide; no smile and ponytail; three class photos taken at corresponding stages; and one photo of the whole school, all hundred and ten of us massed on the playground, the infants sitting cross-legged on gym mats at the front, the teachers on chairs behind them, the rest of the school standing in rows according to seniority, with year five standing on benches at the back.

'I don't know if you'd like these,' said my mother. 'They might amuse Hannah.'

I peered at the school photo. All those faces, of people who had once played a big part in my small life: the bullies, the show-offs, the leaders, the victims, the popular and the despised. The ugly, God help them – what a hard time they had. For all I knew Louella Martin was a supermodel now. And geeky Paul Parfitt, the class boff, could be a civil service mandarin with the ear of the prime minister. And...

My chain of thought snapped. A familiar, muffling silence closed in around me like a mountain fog. I peered more closely at the photograph. My mother's hand appeared, pointing at some other face in the crowd, but if she was making a comment, I couldn't hear it. The girl was there! Unmistakably there in the photograph, standing between me and Avril Wright, her thick dark hair and fierce stare conspicuous between our bland to-order grins. I knew it was impossible, I tried to summon up every rational impulse to banish her, but she remained firmly in place, her eyes holding mine, her powerful presence dominating me, past and present.

'...rather sweet,' my mother was saying, about whoever it was that had caught her eye. 'I remember her being a fast runner, winning things on sports day.'

I sat back. Once again I had that feeling of the here and now breaking over me in a wave, as though my ears had suddenly unblocked and the scales had fallen from my eyes. My breathing and heartbeat rushed and pounded, I was conscious of the blood coursing round my body. The skin on my arms had shrunk into goosebumps, and yet sweat crawled over me beneath my clothes. Each hair on my head seemed separately to stir, making my scalp creep.

'...remember her name?' Julia asked.

'No.'

I glanced back at the photograph, both knowing and dreading what I would – or rather would not – see. The girl had gone.

'...that enormously fat mother, I always

wondered whether the running was a reaction against that ... Fee?'

'Yes?'

'Are you with me, or somewhere else?'

'Sorry,' I said. 'I'm with you.'

'Look, I'm going to put these school ones, and some of the ones of you in another envelope, and you can take them. I've kept those I like, so if you don't want them, just chuck them out.'

'Fine. Thanks Julia.'

I had started the day fired up about my mother's interference and prickly with jealousy over Dean. Now, I was in shock again. In spite of her enquiry I didn't believe my mother had noticed anything. Her nature was to take things at face value. If I said I was fine, then I was fine.

She showed me the service sheets they'd had printed, and described to me the flowers and colour scheme for the wedding breakfast. To all intents and purposes she was the girl, and I the old lady. At midday she drove me over to see the Chantry, a wonderful small chapel in the grounds of a stately home, bought me lunch in the associated National Trust café, and showed me around. It had turned hot again, and I had absolutely no energy; it was all I could do to keep pace with her and make appreciative comments.

When we got back in the car, she said, 'You'll come back, won't you? Tea in the garden? Adrian's coming over at six, I know he'd like to see you.'

'If you don't mind, Julia, I think I'll go home. It's been a lovely day, but I'd quite like to take advantage of a bit of peace and quiet before Hannah gets back – get a few things done, you know how it is.'

'In that case, I shall run you back.'

'But it's miles out of your way, you don't have—'

'Shush! I want to.'

We drove for about ten minutes in silence, and then she put on a CD. Chamber music I think you'd call it – four or five instruments in conversation, civilized and soothing. Like a kind word, the music made my eyes fill with tears. I blinked fast to keep them in, my face turned to the window.

At Arbury Road I asked my mother in, in the expectation that she would refuse, and she didn't let me down.

'No thanks Fee, but I'll leave you to your peace and quiet. And anyway Adrian will be round. But next weekend – the big day!'

I put my hand on her shoulder and kissed her cheek. 'We're really looking forward to it.'

'And you promise you'll go shopping?'

'I promise. Hannah will see to it.'

'*Au revoir*, see you in church!'

I knew the moment I crossed the threshold of the flat that she was there, waiting for me. I realized that I had entered into a sort of collusion with her. An unholy alliance bound us together in our secret universe.

As I entered the living room she was there, plain as day, standing for the first time not close to the wall but in the centre of the room.

'Who are you?' I said. My voice was distant and muffled, my ears blocked once more by the atmospheric bubble she created.

'What do you want?' Now I was shouting, I could feel the force of my voice, in my neck, my face, behind my eyes. 'Why are you here?'

There was no reply, but she seemed, if not to draw closer, to intensify, as though she were trying to communicate through sheer energy; shimmering and trembling like a mirage. Her eyes – those eyes! – were like black holes, sucking me in, her hair a halo of black flames quivering about her white, set face. The room was full of her smell, the stench of stale, secret female blood.

'Go away!' I screamed, and as I did so I felt a gout of my own blood squirt from between my legs, and I fell to my knees, sobbing in panic.

When I dared to look up again she was gone, but the wall bore the mark of her going: her perfect, unambiguous silhouette.

I had come on again; early. Stooped and trembling, like an old woman, I dealt with the blood. When I emerged from the bathroom, I closed the door of the living room and put a chair under the handle. Then I opened the door into the communal hallway and left it propped ajar. That murky chink with its view of peeling wallpaper and junk mail was my security – the assurance that I lived in a building with other people, people who were not mad, haunted or terrified.

I was light-headed and nauseous, but I feared stillness and the space it provided for her to return. No-one who hasn't experienced real terror can know how precious dull, everyday peace can be. I tried to drag it back, to preserve normality by doing normal things. I tidied up, hoovered, did a little ironing; tears running down my face as I spread Hannah's jeans on the board. Moving about the flat I hadn't realized how many reflective surfaces there were in the place – mirrors, pictures, glass-fronted cupboards, and the inward-looking windows around the well ... Wherever I looked I caught sight of her, glaring from behind my shoulder, close enough to touch, but for less than a second. I'd read that ghosts had no reflection, but why wouldn't they? How could I have been stupid enough to imagine I could trap her behind a closed door, when she appeared not just in there, but anywhere she chose? Phil had said it – it was me who was haunted, me she wanted, me she was bearing down on, with her relentless, overpowering need.

When the phone rang, I screamed. It was both a shock and a relief. I pushed over the chair and flung open the living-room door. In spite of the open window the smell was overpowering in here, and after I lifted the handset I gagged and had to put my hand over my mouth.

'Ya-lo?' It was Dean's voice. 'Fee? You there?'

I tried my voice. A little scratch of a voice, like something that had been buried a long, long time. 'Yes.'

'Speak up, the line's terrible.'

I got a grip, cleared my throat. 'Is that better?'

'Yup – look, Fee, we're running a bit late. We went to the pool and picked up a pizza, it'll be more like nine, that okay?'

'No!' I shrieked. 'No, it is not fucking okay! This is the very first time she's been to you on her own and already you're messing me about! I want her back now, do you understand?'

'Fee, sure, but we're just—'

'I don't care what you're fucking well doing, you leave *now*, Dean! This minute!' There was a short pause. My breathing was short and shallow, I was almost sobbing with fear, rage and frustration. 'Dean! I want her home – you're to leave now!'

'Sure, sure, whatever...' His voice took on a placid, soothing tone. In my panic-stricken state I suspected that he was only humouring me, saying that he would come when in reality he would take his time.

'How long does it take?' I shouted. 'The drive – how long?'

'I dunno, I've never done it direct—'

'You must have some idea! Half an hour?'

''Bout that. Bit more perhaps.'

I looked at my watch, which said six thirty. 'If you're not back by seven thirty she's never coming to you again! Got that?'

'Got it.'

'So do it! Do it now, she can eat the fucking pizza in the car, or eat when she gets home, or she can bloody starve, but I want to see her in this flat in under an hour!'

'Settle down, Fee!' Now he did sound genuinely taken aback. 'I told you, you got it. See you.'

This was followed by a measured *click*. I slammed the handset down and stood there, jolted by noisy gut-wrenching sobs.

I couldn't stay in the flat. I picked up my keys and the envelope containing the photographs, and walked out. I would go to the dusty little garden at the end of the road and sit on a bench for a while. People would take me for one of the local derelicts – shuffling, muttering, wild-eyed, a head case – and they'd be right.

As I emerged into the hall, I saw one of the other tenants, a young man I'd seen a couple of times before, riffling through a handful of post. He glanced up at me and I could tell at once that he had heard me on the phone, through the open door.

'Evening,' he said. 'All right?'

It was a formulaic greeting, but my reply wasn't. 'Why shouldn't I be?'

'Hey—' He held up the hand holding the letters. 'No offence.'

I slammed my own door, ostentatiously testing the lock. The young man dropped most of the letters back on the floor and loped up the staircase two at a time, crouching forward, like an ape.

The little garden was where I'd sat before, on the day of the thunderstorm – the day when she'd followed me into St Agnes and waited, patiently, by the door. I sat on the bench nearest the entrance. At twenty to seven it was still hot. I knew I had to be back by seven because it would be just like Dean to drive flat out and do the journey in less than half an hour just to show me – I would look both ridiculous and irresponsible if I was out when he got there.

I had brought the photographs as a displacement activity, so that I wouldn't be sitting there staring into space. As I pulled out the first pictures the small brown envelope, softened and creased with age, fluttered to the ground at my feet.

I picked it up, and opened it. For a

moment I thought it was empty, then I saw the gleam of shiny paper in one corner. It was a piece of cellophane, folded in four; it was protecting a tiny, silken curl of black hair.

Seventeen

'Really?' said my mother. 'It must be yours.'

'No,' I said. 'I was fair as a child, and bald as a baby. You've always told me.'

'A mystery!' she declared. But there was something shrill in her tone. She may not actually have been lying, but she was concealing something. Not just from me, but from herself.

'Julia,' I said. 'You *must* try and remember. Please. It's more important than you know.'

'Now you are getting me worried!' She gave a bright, high laugh. 'Don't worry, I'll do my best.'

'Thank you.'

'Is Hannah back yet?'

'No. I'm expecting her any minute.'

'Give her a big kiss from me.'

'I will – Julia, they're here, I must go. Please try to remember about the lock of hair!'

All through this conversation I'd kept my eyes closed, but I knew I was being watched, and listened to. I could feel the girl's attention pressing on me intently. Every so often I was assailed by a wave of her hot, sickly, intimate smell, as if she were suddenly very close, her face next to mine. Now, I put the phone down firmly, and hurried out on to the pavement, looking neither to right nor left, leaving both doors on the latch. I was sweating. Dean would never know how badly I needed Hannah with me.

The jeep was parked alongside the residents' parking bay, hazard lights flashing – Dean was busy conveying an air of urgency. The two front doors flapped open and he slammed his and came round to relieve Hannah of her purple rucksack and help her jump down.

As soon as he saw me he glanced at his watch, then tilted his wrist towards me. 'This do you?'

I ignored him and addressed Hannah. 'Hallo darling, good day?'

'Mum!' She kissed me enthusiastically which was both unusual and nice, except I suspected I was merely the beneficiary of Dean's spoiling. I tried to remind myself that this wasn't about me.

'It was well cool! We—'

'Do you want to come in for a bit?' I asked.

'No can do,' said Dean, probably the last man on earth to use the phrase without irony – or at all. 'She's all fed and watered. Bye princess.'

'Bye—' She allowed him to kiss her.

'What do you say?' I prompted.

'Thanks for a lovely day.'

'It was my pleasure. We'll do it again, yeah?'

She nodded vigorously, not meeting his eye. Her innate decency nearly broke my heart. Dean looked at me over her head and I could tell, with a pang, that he was affected too. He was starting to love her – who wouldn't?

'I'll give a bell,' he said. 'Fix up another meet.'

'Yes.'

'Cheers then.'

'Bye Dean.'

With Hannah I was safe. She'd eaten, so I made myself a sandwich and ate it with her in the living room while we watched the latest episode of a hospital drama. She showed no desire to debrief. Maybe she was being discreet, but I think it was mainly a nine-year-old's natural tendency to move in the present. Whatever the reason, I didn't press her. The details of the day would come out in dribs and drabs during the week.

When the programme was over, I told her what I'd been doing, and the plans for Julia's wedding. Just like my mother, she immediately asked when we were going shopping.

'Tomorrow? All the shops will be open.'

'Yay!'

She reacted with healthy disrespect, and some hilarity, to the old photographs, especially the ones of me in my ruched swimsuit and sunhat ... Julia's first wedding, though, she approved of, studying it closely without the merest snigger.

'Granny was really pretty!'

'She still is.'

'Her skirt's really short.'

'That was the fashion. And the long hair.'

'What can I get to wear?'

'What sort of thing would you like?'

'A denim mini-skirt – with sparkles.'

It was perfectly clear she'd given this matter a good deal of thought and this was her firm and considered conclusion. Well, she was a modern nine-year-old of strong opinions, Julia surely wouldn't expect her to be in French smocking and Mary Janes.

'We'll see what we can find,' I said, and was rewarded with a hug – cupboard love, but still welcome.

When we'd made a preliminary selection of which photos we might want to put in an album, I replaced them in the envelope. As I did so, the lock of hair, which had somehow come adrift from its packaging, drifted to the floor. Hannah spotted it, and before I could stop her, picked it up.

'Look, it's someone's hair!'

'So it is. Pop it back in and we'll make sure Granny—'

'Whose is it?'

'I've no idea.'

Hannah held the curl so close to her face that she was almost squinting, and stroked it between her finger and thumb.

'It's so, so silky ... It's baby hair.'

'You think?' I held out my hand for it, but she seemed not to notice, continuing to peer and stroke.

'Not yours, though ... Which baby?' Her voice had sunk to a whisper. 'Which baby?' The whisper was so resonant, so sibilant that it seemed to come not just from Hannah's mouth, but from everywhere, from the air

266

itself.

Which baby? Which baby?

I could actually feel the breath of that whisper on my cheek, like a draught, and with it that shockingly familiar smell.

'Hannah!'

'What?' I had shouted, and she looked and sounded aggrieved, as well she might.

'Give me that!'

'Okay, okay, go on then.' She tried to throw the lock of hair at me but it was too light and simply floated on to the sofa cushion between us. She got up and the movement caused it to flutter to the ground, so that even as I tried to call her back I was scrabbling around for it.

'Hannah—'

'I'm going to bed.'

'So am I! I'm just coming.'

'Whatever...'

I put the hair back in the envelope, closed the window and the door and practically ran down the corridor to the bedroom. Her clothes were on the floor and she was already dragging her pony T-shirt over her head; her face, when it emerged from the neck of the T-shirt, framed by flattened hair, wore the pinched, closed expression I hated.

'Hannah, darling, I'm sorry – I wasn't

cross.'

'You were.' She got into bed and turned, with a flounce of the duvet, on to her side with her back to me. 'You...' She muttered something I couldn't catch.

'What's that?' I went and sat on the edge of the bed, putting my hand on her shoulder but she shook me off with a convulsive twitch.

'Nothing.'

In a flash, I decided I was being too apologetic. She was a kid, after all. I was the adult. My only crime was to have raised my voice for a moment at the end of a long day, while all over London children, some of them much younger than Hannah were being beaten, neglected, starved and physically, mentally and sexually abused. She was a loved, cared for and largely indulged little girl, and I was entitled to an off moment.

I got up. 'Anyway,' I said. 'We'll forget about teeth-cleaning for tonight.' This was said to remind her of my authority, and the power it gave me to set, and to waive, certain rules. But she didn't favour me with a response. I went and cleaned my own teeth, being careful not to look in the mirror, and returned to the bedroom.

'Night,' I said as I got in to bed.

There was a long silence. I picked up my book, found my place, and began gazing sightlessly at the print.

Her voice when it finally came from behind the screen was so faint, so ethereally unemphatic that no-one but me would have heard it.

'Night...'

Adult I may have been, but my eyes filled with warm tears of relief.

'Sleep well,' I said. 'See you in the morning.'

I read for a while after that. I was always more at ease in here, and the peace of rapprochement hung in the air along with Hannah's gentle breathing. Also, I liked the view of the sky through the glass above me. I clung to the comforting thought that the same sky, the same stars, hung over everyone and my fears were nothing by comparison. Whether or not I deserved to be, I was in His hands.

I must have fallen asleep over my book, because when I woke it was three a.m. and the bedside lamp was still on. I put the book on the floor, slid down on the pillows, reached out and switched off the lamp. The effect of this was to make the area of the skylight seem lighter than the room where I lay. So I saw at once the dark shape of something up there, moving slowly and painfully – half crawling, half slithering – across the glass. The only animal capable of being up there was a cat, but this was much bigger than any cat. Nor did it move with a cat's sure-footed grace. I was hypnotized by the thing's creeping, clinging progress. It seemed both helpless and horrifying, I wanted to turn away, but couldn't. I lay pinned to the bed in fear staring upwards, trapped again by that thick, muffling silence. Whatever it was it made no sound.

Now it had almost reached the other side and I prepared myself for its disappearance as it continued on its way along the uneven shadowed canyon between the terraces. And indeed it did disappear, but only for a second. Perhaps it had sensed me watching, for it turned back, and there was her face, white, black-eyed, desperate, staring down at me.

How had she got there? I must have made some sound, for I woke Hannah.

'Mum...?' I could hear the almost-crying, baby-like fear in her voice. But at least it cut through the shroud of silence. I turned on the lamp.

'It's all right!' I did my best, but my voice still quavered.

'What's the matter?' She appeared round the screen, looking at me warily from a distance.

'Nothing, darling, honestly. I must have been having a bad dream. Come and give us a kiss.'

She shook her head. 'No it's okay.' She thought the kiss was to comfort her, she couldn't know that I wasn't offering, but asking. I entertained a flash of memory, of the two of us arriving at this flat three months ago, me clinging to my daughter's hand for comfort.

'Back to bed then,' I said.

She gave me a last suspicious look and then I heard the rustle and flop of the bedclothes as she snuggled down.

I hoped she couldn't hear my convulsive shaking. I kept the lamp on, and my eyes open, till dawn.

The next day I told Hannah that we were definitely going shopping, as promised, but that we were going to church first.

'*What?*' Her goggle-eyed astonishment was perfectly justifiable, in view of the fact that she had had no contact whatever with organized religion – at least through me – in her entire life. The next question followed as the night the day. '*Why?*'

I opted for the simple truth, but not the whole of it. 'I just want to,' I said. 'I feel like it – if you don't mind.'

'I suppose.' Bafflement was in the ascendancy over outrage, *pro tem*, and I took advantage.

'You don't have to come. If Meriel's there, perhaps you could stay with her.'

'But Olwyn goes,' said Hannah gloomily. 'So we won't be able to.'

'Let's see.'

As it turned out, Olwyn was 'skiving' as she put it, doing some work in the garden, and was perfectly happy for Meriel to skip Sunday school and play with Hannah.

'Phil will be delighted,' she said. 'You'll swell his congregation by about ten per cent.'

I hadn't even thought to ask what sort of service I was in for, and felt slightly sheepish when it turned out to be parish communion. I wasn't confirmed, didn't know the order of service or the prayers, and only recognized one of the hymns and that only because I remembered it from school. Thank heavens Phil had the sense not to make any references to welcoming newcomers, and my eight fellow worshippers were very friendly but reserved. I think they were almost as embarrassed as me, perhaps imagining me to be some deanery spy, or mad evangelical who might raise her arms to heaven and speak in tongues at any moment. They needn't have worried. I sat very still, kept my head down, put a fiver in the bag because I had nothing smaller, and was a model of humble self-effacement.

Phil preached on the theme of humility. It was a good sermon, well delivered though there was no-one present, including myself, who looked in the least puffed-up. A little later, he said something about everyone being welcome at the altar when communion was being dished out, and to take your prayer book if you only wanted a blessing. I nearly chickened out – I was sure I was the only one not properly churched – but at the last moment I got to my feet, reminding myself that I needed every blessing I could get. Phil's hand on my head was warm and reassuring.

At the end of the service the woman collecting the books said how nice it was to see me and asked me where I lived.

'So you've come a long way!'

'I know Phil,' I explained. I thought this might sound like a rather poor reason for attending, but she seemed more than satisfied.

'He's absolutely wonderful. He and Olwyn are the best thing that's happened to St Mary's in years.'

Phil was doing his stuff in the porch, and I hung back so as to be last in the queue.

'Greetings!' He kissed me heartily on the cheek as if it were a social occasion. 'Nice to see you. Coffee back at the ranch?'

'I'll walk back with you, but I have to take Hannah shopping.'

'Then you'll need fortifying. Hang on while I get into my civvies.'

He returned wearing a short-sleeved shirt and black trousers, his 'uniform' over his arm, and closed the heavy door firmly behind him.

'How is everything?' he asked, 'Any particular reason for your being here this morning?'

'Not good,' I replied. 'And yes.'

'I'm sorry.'

'It's not your fault.'

'I know. And you wouldn't be here if you

274

hadn't taken some comfort from the proceedings.'

'No,' I admitted.

On the short walk to the vicarage, he asked: 'Any luck on the story front? Anything come to light?'

I was about to say no, but then remembered something. 'Possibly. It might have done. But whether there's any connection...'

'Who knows?' he said, opening the gate for me. 'But I tell you one thing, this isn't going to last for ever. It's a process, and it will proceed to its conclusion.'

'That's what I'm afraid of.'

'God's on your side, Fee. There's nothing to be afraid of.'

After the terror of the night before – the terror that was my constant companion, stalking and shadowing me, ready to put out its hand and claim me anywhere, at any time – it was difficult to share his confidence. But I was still glad I'd gone, to be touched by others' beliefs and certainties, even if I had none of my own.

Hannah and I went to Topshop and shopped up a storm at Julia's expense, though probably not to her taste. Hannah found the sparkly denim skirt of her dreams, and a pretty embroidered gypsy top and slouchy boots to go with it. I accompanied her on the ethnic route, with a dark blue tiered skirt, white ruffled blouse, blue ribbon espadrilles and a floppy hat. We were still well under budget so we picked up some fun jewellery and a couple of skinny scarves as well. All this on the basis that there would be more than enough tailored elegance around on the day, so we might as well cut a boho dash.

We ate – I suppose you'd call it lunch, though it was three o'clock when we sat down – with touristy types in a cheap and cheerful pasta joint near the Post Office Tower. It was gone four when we emerged, but I couldn't face going home. In fact I could hardly bear to be still, for fear of being tracked down, for fear of what might happen. Hannah was the beneficiary of my unease, because we tramped to the nearest multiplex and found a five o'clock showing of a PG-rated romantic comedy about a couple brought together by their pets, and that saw us through till seven, when she was beginning to flag.

'Mum, I'm knackered. Can we go home?'

Poor child, exhausted by fashion and fun. A bus was coming, so we hopped on that rather than the much faster tube – I needed the light.

I was so, so glad Hannah was with me. The moment I opened our front door she was in there, kicking off her trainers and asking if she could call Meriel with an inventory of her purchases. But as I followed her, stiff with apprehension, into the living room it was full of Mark's voice, leaving a message.

'...so anyway, here I am, back from foreign parts and I can't wait—'

I snatched up the handset. 'Mark?'

'Hallo!'

Hannah was making frantic 'Hurry-up-*I*-want-to' faces at me, but I waved her away and she retreated contentedly with her carrier bags.

'Fee? You there?'

'Yes! Oh yes, you have no idea how wonderful it is to hear your voice.'

'Good. Ditto.' He sounded gratified, if slightly puzzled. 'Can I come round?'

'Well...' I pondered. 'Hannah's here—'

'Then I suppose I shall have to keep my baser nature in check. Look, I want to see you. I'll be good as gold.'

'You know where we are. Come over at half past eight, Hannah should be asleep then.'

It was so good to see him. So much better, just for a moment, to be in his arms than in God's hands.

'How's it going?' he asked, after we'd waited interminably for Hannah to fall asleep, and re-established contact with thrilling studenty discomfort on the living room sofa bed. 'Have you experienced any more nasties?'

I hesitated, knowing this was a test, and that I had two options: I could take the line of least resistance and make light of all that had happened in his absence; or I could level with him and risk a re-run of our earlier contretemps.

'Yes,' I said, 'I have.'

I told him everything, as calmly as I could, including my visit to church that morning. He listened intently, gazing at point-blank range into my face as we lay entwined on the sofa, occasionally brushing my cheek with his fingers, as if checking for tears. When I'd finished, he said, 'Poor darling, it must be terrifying. Is there anything I can do?'

I shook my head, but now I did shed a few tears, because he had already done the most important thing, which was to let me know he was on my side.

He kissed me and held me tight. I knew nothing could touch or hurt me if I had the love and understanding of this man – this particular man.

'So what happens next?' he asked. 'If, as Phil says, this is a process, with its own inevitable conclusion, does that mean you simply have to endure it till it's over?'

'I'm not sure.'

'Because if so, I shall regard it as my duty to move in and protect you.'

He snuggled lecherously against me, and that made me laugh. 'For heaven's sake, what about Reuben?'

'Oh yes, I'd forgotten about him. I'd have to have a double life, move back every other weekend.'

I'd told him about the lock of hair, and I then said, as if outlining a plan although in fact I'd only just thought about it, 'I need to talk to my mother again.'

A little later, he whispered, 'Can I stay, just for tonight?'

'No! Hannah sleeps in the same room!'

'In here, silly. Nothing the matter with this.'

'I don't know what she'd make of it...'

'She doesn't have to make anything of it!'

He wrapped his arms round me, stifling my protests in a hug of passionate exasperation. 'I'm a friend, you put me up for the night. If she has a precociously smutty mind there's nothing you or I can do about it.'

He stayed. And I stayed with him until the small hours, when I crept back along the passage and into bed. I left the lamp off, didn't look up, and slept the sleep of the laid.

In the morning Hannah took his presence in her stride, and he left the flat long before us, whispering 'love you' in my ear as he went. I made a couple of phone calls before we set off – one to Olwyn to ask if, yet again, Hannah could go there after school, and another to my mother. I didn't tell her why I wanted to visit, and it wasn't her style to ask.

'Yes, lovely,' she said. 'You can show me what you bought.'

Julia was nobody's fool, and made no comment when I arrived empty-handed. I refused a glass of wine, but she poured herself one and took me into the garden. To my horror Adrian was there – why wouldn't he be? – but he had the good sense to announce that, actually, he was just going.

'One of the advantages of a mature

relationship,' he said in his droll, toffish way. 'Two centres of operation – always somewhere to retreat to.'

She went with him to the door and there was a brief, intimate pause before it was closed behind him. When she came back she was shiny-bright, and I dreaded what I had to say.

'Julia – I've got to ask you something.'

'I know.'

For a moment I wasn't sure I'd heard her. 'Sorry?'

'I haven't forgotten, Fee. You want to know about the lock of hair.'

I thought: *She's had a secret, and now she's going to tell me. At last.*

'Yes,' I said. 'I do.'

She put down her glass and folded her arms, raised one elegant sandalled foot and gazed at it. Then looked away for a second. A sequence of little preparatory rituals. With hindsight I can appreciate how frightened she must have been; it took enormous courage for someone like her to tell me what she did, especially when, as far as she knew, she was revealing so much of her most intimate history for the first time.

I waited patiently, respectfully even, until she was ready.

'You aren't going to like all this, Fee,' she said. 'I hoped never to have to tell you. It's not something I wanted you to carry.'

For a moment it was all on the tip of my tongue, but I managed to keep quiet.

'One thing you should know first, and never forget, is that I truly loved your father.'

'You told me that before,' I said curtly. 'After the funeral.'

'He was – very lovable. Well, you remember.'

'I suppose.' Already, I was grudging. The premonitory signs were there.

'You asked me then if he was good to me.'

'And you wouldn't answer.'

She didn't rise to this. 'Most of the time he was. But not always. There was something in him – a demon. A besetting sin. He had a temper he couldn't control.' She looked at me. Her arms were still crossed, and her fingers were white, digging into her arms. The look she gave me dared me to ask for more, but it only fuelled the old, rotten anger inside me.

'So what exactly are you saying?' I asked. 'That he treated you badly?'

'Sometimes...' She cleared her throat. 'From time to time.'

'How badly?'

'He did ... hit me. He couldn't help it.' I opened my mouth in outrage, but she held up her hand. 'It's the story we've all read about. He hit me, he was remorseful, I forgave him, we carried on till the next time. I was a very, very stupid woman.'

'No, Julia,' I said pointedly. 'You weren't stupid.'

'It used to come in waves,' she went on, 'it was cyclical. Probably, if he could have been persuaded to go to a doctor, there would have been some medication that might have helped—'

'Don't excuse him!' I could hear my voice rising dangerously. 'What he did was inexcusable, and unforgivable. You can love him all you like. I hate him!'

If I shocked myself with this outburst, I was gratified to see that I'd shocked her even more. She was white as a sheet. 'Fee, please – it's all over, he's dead.'

'Good fucking riddance!'

'Don't swear! Don't! I won't have it!'

She was as close to tears as I'd ever seen her, but for some reason this enraged me even more. To turn the taps on now, over some perceived minor impropriety, when for all those years she had covered up, and pretended, and suffered in silence and in secret for propriety's sake.

'You won't have it?' I snarled sarcastically. 'It's a bit late for that, surely.'

There was a split-second pause as she took this in. At once, with the tears still on her face, she was cool again. 'I don't understand you. What do you mean, late?'

I should have known that nothing would get past her, even under cover of my bluster, but her perceptiveness just made me more angry and I blundered on, laying about me, knowing the damage I was doing to her, and to my cause. 'You took all that shit for years, Julia! You were prepared to "have" that, as you so quaintly put it, and cover up for Dad just because of appearances, so what makes a bit of swearing so shocking?'

She raised her eyebrows. 'I'm not shocked. But you can hardly blame me for wanting to maintain the civilities.'

'I can!' I snapped. 'I do! Do you have any idea what it was like living with all that going on? Being your fellow conspirator? I was only a kid, for God's sake!'

'What?'

Too late, I realized that I had given myself away. I shall never forget the expression on her face; blank and pallid, like a net curtain, behind which all the furniture of her past life, or her perception of it, was being summarily, brutally repossessed.

As for me, I was in too deep to get out. I probably owed Julia an apology, but instead was hell-bent on trying to exact one from her. The purpose of this visit was lost, blown away in the firestorm of thirty years of pent-up resentment.

'Did you honestly think I didn't know? That I wouldn't find out? Parents are a child's whole world, and you and Dad were busy knocking the foundations out of it night after night.'

There were all kinds of things wrong about this accusation but she chose to ignore them, and instead to state the simple truth. 'I was trying to protect you.'

'Well,' I said, with all the wild cruelty at my disposal, 'you failed.'

'I see.'

I was frightened of the silence rising around us, and what it contained. I stood up, and found that my legs were shaking.

'Yes,' said Julia, rising. 'It's probably best if you go.' She gave a twitch of a smile. 'You've given me rather a lot to think about.'

Whenever in future years I looked back on that little scene it always called to mind that famous quotation on the conduct of Charles

I on the gallows: *He nothing common did or mean, upon that memorable scene* ... It was my mother's finest hour, and my most despicable. I can't remember if she saw me out, I didn't even close the door behind me. I stormed down the road blinded by tears of rage and self-pity. Did she weep? To my eternal shame, I still don't know.

Eighteen

When you hate yourself as much as I did after that, it takes a while to recalibrate. Self-loathing needs a scapegoat, you have to convince yourself that others are at least as loathsome as you. Saying sorry is therefore not an option. You might as well go on being vile to justify how you feel.

I collected Hannah – for the simple, selfish reason that I wanted someone with me at the flat – and was so snappy and short-tempered with her that I had no trouble getting her to bed early. Mark called but I told him not to come round, despite his agonized entreaties. I longed to see him, but one thing self-hatred is not, is sexy.

There was no peace. How could there be? She was distraught, her misery and anger beat at the silence with frantic wings, her smell brought the bile into my mouth so that I couldn't eat, she was at my side every moment so that wherever I moved I brushed against her. When at last I got in to bed I closed my eyes tight and drew the bedclothes over my face. I would not look, because I knew what I would see. She was so close, so wretched, so ferociously helpless – I had let her down.

After an age, I slept. But at about three thirty I was aware of a small sound, as though an animal had crept on to my pillow: the tiny, guttural creaks and sniffs of un-vocalized weeping, a dampness on my cheek ... The secrecy of it was heartbreaking. Now she was trying *not* to disturb me, these were the real tears of a particular child, and I was the cause of them.

Next morning Hannah was sulky and sleepy-eyed. 'You were talking in your sleep,' she said accusingly. 'Can you stop doing that?'

* * *

'Okay, what's up?' asked Anita when I got to work.

'Nothing, really.'

'Fine – that explains the red-eye and the face like a smacked arse, then.'

'I had a row with my mother.'

'Sounds healthy to me,' she said. 'Who won?'

'No-one.'

'That figures. There are no winners in a war. Coffee?'

'Thanks.'

She led the way into the back room, turfing Kenny out to mind the shop.

'Nothing private, mate, we just don't want you listening in.'

'I know when I'm not wanted.'

'Sweetie, it's the only reason I hired you.'

This little exchange was without acrimony, a sort of accepted office by-play. Kenny cleared off and Anita made coffee.

'So,' she said. 'It's a case of who gets off their high horse first, right?'

Anita's wire-wool-and-carbolic approach to counselling made it easier to admit the truth. 'She's not on hers, actually. Though she'd have every right to be.'

'But you're on yours because you're in the wrong.'

'Something like that.'

'What a bugger...' she agreed. 'And doesn't she get married in a few days time? But don't worry. Climbing down's not so bad, when you're ready.'

When I was ready – that was the catch. The hours were ticking by towards my mother's wedding, and I had walked out on her in the worst possible way. The clothes we had bought hung on the back of the bedroom door like a reproach. If I was to be there, wishing her well, something had to give.

Besides, I was seeing the girl everywhere now. I glimpsed her in the street, in the office, in shops, in the park, scorching me with that glare of frantic, miserable re-proach. In the flat she all but suffocated me with her attention. Hannah caught me try-ing to push her away in the kitchen, and said, 'Mum – what are you doing?'

'Making supper.'

'No, flapping like that, you looked really weird.'

'There was a wasp.'

She wrinkled her nose in distaste. 'Any-way, what are you cooking? There's a funny smell in here.'

'I hadn't noticed.'

That got the 'yeah, right' treatment.

I had been keeping Mark at arm's length, but that night he turned up and I fell into his arms, a weeping wreck. It was the first time Hannah had witnessed the clear proof that he was more than just a friend, and her face was a study, but I was past caring. To his eternal credit Mark hit the right note, by saying to her, over my shuddering shoulders: 'Your mum's a bit down, we need to tell her we love her, a lot.'

'She's been weird,' Hannah said, as he sat me down on the sofa. 'She talked in her sleep again.'

'Is that right? Was it interesting?'

Fortunately both Hannah and I said 'No' at the same time, she qualifying hers with: 'It was just, like, nonsense.'

'Well,' said Mark, 'I'm going to spend the night here tonight, right here on this sofa, and I shall keep an eye on things, so you can both sleep tight.'

I crept along and joined him when Hannah was asleep, but as I lay wrapped in his arms I could see her standing in the middle of the room, staring at us, telling me unequivocally that there was to be no escape.

Mark's whispered small-hours advice was the same as Anita's. 'Say sorry. It'll only take a second and everything will be fine. Just think what a great day the wedding will be if all this is behind you.'

He was right and I knew it. Back in my own bed I resolved that it would be the first thing I did next day, even if it meant Hannah being late for school.

At seven a.m. Mark shook me awake and passed me the handset.

'Thought I'd better not answer.'

Groggily I rolled on to my back. 'Hallo...'

'Fee, it's me. Julia.'

I pulled myself up. 'Hallo.'

'I wanted to say sorry.'

She had beaten me to it, but the relief was so intense that my head swam, and I covered my eyes with my hand.

'Me too. With far more reason.'

'No – no. Let's not have a guilt competition. But can we try again? I have the strong sense of a deadline. Adrian doesn't know any of these things, and may never know. But I want to say "I do" knowing that you and I have cleared the decks.'

Cleared the decks – that was a very Julia expression. Hannah appeared round the screen, rubbing and scratching accusingly and I pointed in the direction of the kitchen, and mouthed 'Mark'.

'I could come today,' I said.

'I shall be here.'

Mark drove Hannah and me to school, and then took me on to my mother's. It was another beautiful morning, but I was shivering as he kissed me good-bye.

'Hey – brace up. This is all good.'

'I'm frightened.'

'But afterwards, you won't be.'

Julia opened the door as I approached, and waved to Mark. When the door closed behind us she embraced me lightly, and we exchanged a cautious kiss – we had never been tactile with one another, so it felt new, and strange, a renegotiation of our relationship.

'Thank you for coming.'

'Please...' I took a breath and spat it out. 'I've been in hell, actually.'

She touched my arm without looking at me.

We sat in the garden in exactly the same chairs as we had the other day. I knew that this was deliberate, part of her plan to close the wound and continue, seamlessly, from where we had left off.

'How shall we start?' she asked.

'You go. I'll listen.'

'And you won't – you'll hear me out?'

'Yes.'

'Very well then. These – these episodes, I suppose you'd call them nowadays – they happened. And I was saved having to make a decision because in the end your father tired of me and left of his own accord. He found someone else, as you know, and as far as I'm aware he didn't mistreat her, so you can make of that what you will – no, I don't want to hear your theory, Fee.' She bent and plucked a blade of grass, which she held between finger and thumb, in her lap, gazing down at it as though it held the secrets of the universe.

'You're absolutely right,' she said quietly. 'The lock of hair isn't yours.'

She cleared her throat, rolling the blade of grass between her finger and thumb. I waited. Now, it was coming. The silence was thick, pregnant, a mixture of anticipation and foreboding. It was a silence that only Julia could, or should, break. And – no, I wasn't imagining it – there was the merest trace of that smell in the air. She was with us. She, and I, were about to find out what we most wanted and needed to know.

'It was your sister's,' said Julia.

Yes.

'Just after your tenth birthday your father went through a bad patch. He attacked me several times in one week. Unfortunately, as a result, I got pregnant.'

Sister ... Sister...

'I didn't tell Miles. He didn't touch me for ages after that and I got through to my seventh month without either you or Miles knowing. But then the baby stopped moving. I went to St Mary's and they told me the baby had died. I had to have an induced still-birth...'

Oh God, oh God, oh God.

'They're very good about it, you're encouraged to sit holding the baby for as long as you want, to treat it like a real person. Which she was.'

She was.

'Like you she was a pretty baby. Very small of course, premature, but with wonderful black hair. They rinsed the sticky stuff off her and I snipped off that tiny piece. After an hour or so they took her away. I came home. I remember we had smoked trout for supper. Your father was exceptionally sweet. I'd told him I was going in to hospital for tests for suspected fibroids, and he was terrified I'd be asked about the marks. But I would never have said anything, and he was grateful for that. In a way. Resentful, too. No one likes to be under an obligation, especially a man like Miles. That's proba ly why he went in the end.' She glanced up at me. 'It was all extremely complicated, y u see.'

She is.

For the first time I fully understood the expression 'a full heart' – my own was brimming, bursting. With difficulty, I found my voice, and forced it out through the clinging silence between us. It took an enormous effort, as if all my physical and mental strength were focused on this one act of breaching the invisible wall of time, and shame, and secrecy.

'Did you give her a name?'

'Grace.'

Grace.

The single syllable dropped, sweet and cool into the silence, like the first raindrop after heat. At last, a name. An acknowledgement. An answer. The single drop that made my too-full heart overflow, and the healing tears run down my cheeks.

Grace...

The room began to clear, the atmosphere to change, and freshen. Not in the sudden, violent, interrupted way that it had done before when she had been close, and frightened away, but as if she were gently leaving us ... Withdrawing of her own accord.

'Grace,' I said. I spoke it, like a prayer: 'Grace.'

My mother, like me, was weeping. Sitting still, her glass between her hands, the tears slipping down her cheeks.

'I'm sorry, Fee ... I'm so terribly, terribly sorry...'

I went and kneeled in front of her, took the glass away, and held both her hands in mine.

'No,' I said, 'don't be, not about this. You have nothing to be sorry for.'

She was sobbing, she pulled her hands away and covered her face, rocking from side to side. 'What must you think of me? I've taken away your childhood!'

I found, incredibly, that I was smiling. How astonishing that she could think that, when she had just given me so much. Given me, in every sense, Grace.

'You haven't taken away anything,' I said. 'You've done something absolutely wonderful, you don't know how wonderful. And you were so brave – I could never be that brave!'

She wiped at her eyes and peered at me. I nodded, and held her; our second embrace.

For a moment our roles were reversed. She was slender as a child herself, but so resilient. I felt her arms move cautiously, carefully, followed a second later by the light touch of her hands on my back.

When we drew apart she was more composed, which was right – I was glad she had become her old self again. We had our way of doing things, and it worked. Everything had changed, but would continue the same.

'So you forgive me?' she asked.

'There's nothing to forgive.'

'I had secrets.'

'Everyone does. And you were protecting me, you said so yourself. But I don't need protecting any more. You don't know how pleased, how happy I am to know about Grace. And she would be pleased too – to be remembered, after all this time.'

Julia brushed at her tears. 'That's true.' She leaned forward, her hands clasped as if in prayer. 'And what about your father?'

Phil would have been proud of me.

'He doesn't need us,' I said. 'He's forgiven anyway.'

At the door we embraced for a third time, standing carefully within the circle of each other's arms, testing our new feelings.

When we stood back, she said: 'Fee – if there's someone you'd like to bring to the wedding, please do. They'd be very welcome. The man you've been seeing...?'

'Thank you. His name's Mark.'

'Hannah wouldn't mind?'

'I'll ask her.'

We didn't touch again, but as she opened the door for me she said, almost to herself, 'My darling daughter...'

She might have meant me, or Grace. It didn't matter.

When we got home that evening I was so tired I could hardly keep my eyes open. But it was a good tiredness – as if I'd climbed a mountain, or run the length of a beach. I knew already how well and peacefully I'd sleep.

A 'by hand' note lay on the doormat, with just the number of the flat on the envelope. It was from the students next door. They'd discovered a faulty joint in one of their pipes, apparently, and were having it put right.

And there were three messages on the answerphone, one from Dean, another from Mark. The third one was from Anita, asking for my mother's address – she and Janine wanted to send a card.

I told Hannah to call her father, and then pass him over. I'd speak to Mark later. I wanted him to come with me to my mother's wedding.

Nineteen

My mother's wedding, in the still, numinous space of the Chantry, was memorable for many reasons.

It was memorable for the beauty, elegance and composure of the bride, outshining all of us in her seventh decade and her bright new marriage.

For the gentle, handsome groom who could not take his eyes off her.

For the sound, sophisticated affection of their few good friends.

For Hannah in her sparkling clothes, high on excitement and Buck's Fizz, darting and calling like a tropical bird.

For Mark, standing next to me and touching my hand for a secret second during the marriage vows.

For me – changed, vulnerable, still emerging from my shell into a fresh and altered world.

And most of all for Grace, who had restored me to my mother, and she to me, and whose spirit was still there in the measured music, the scent of flowers, the voices warm with love.

My amazing Grace ... My sister.

One Sunday afternoon in early October, Mark and I took the children to the park. You couldn't quite have described Reuben and Hannah as friends, not yet, but they could get along fine for short periods, and we were working on it. At home, the computer was their lightning-conductor, a helpful shared focus. Out here, freed up by space, and dogs, and other children, they larked about unselfconsciously, orbiting us as we walked, shrieking and skirmishing.

It was beautiful autumn weather, the slight closing-in of the afternoon pressing golden light through bronze and amber leaves, and making a dazzle on the water of the lake. Mark and I walked arm in arm, sure of each other but not of the future, happy to go with the flow.

On the way back, we stopped for a while at

the play area, and sat on a bench while the kids had a go on things. It was just beginning to get chilly, and we huddled together, but the wonderful low light cast romantic shadows, and the children's voices were like birdcalls in the peculiarly resonant London air.

And then it got very quiet. Not oppressively silent, but peaceful. The ground in the play area was covered with a thick carpet of wood-chips, so you couldn't hear footsteps, and maybe whatever wind there was had gone round so the chirruping voices no longer carried.

At any rate, it was a lovely quietness, and that was when I saw her – a tall, dark woman of about thirty, helping Hannah on to the first rung of the rope ladder. There was something especially graceful and caring in her movements, she inspired trust. I found myself smiling as I watched her. Then Hannah was on her way, and the woman turned to look at me, as if she knew I was there.

She smiled, and I knew at once who it was. And that I wouldn't see her again.

Then Hannah called: 'Mum! Look at me! I got to the top!' And I looked instead at my daughter, waving and shouting from her place at the top of the ladder.